CONTEMPORARY AMERICAN FICTION
THE SORCERER'S APPRENTICE

Charles Johnson is the author of *Faith and the Good Thing, Oxherding Tale, Being and Race: Black Writing Since 1970,* and *Middle Passage,* which won the 1990 National Book Award. He is Pollock Professor of English at the University of Washington, a Guggenheim Fellow, a National Book Award judge, a monthly reviewer for *The Los Angeles Times,* and consulting editor for *The Seattle Review.* He has received the Writers Guild Award for his PBS drama, "Booker," lectured internationally for the U.S. Information Agency, published numerous critical articles, written for many television series, and was named by a recent survey conducted by the University of Southern California to be one of the ten best short story writers in America.

THE SORCERER'S APPRENTICE

CHARLES JOHNSON

PENGUIN BOOKS

PENGUIN BOOKS
Published by the Penguin Group
Viking Penguin, a division of Penguin Books USA Inc.,
375 Hudson Street, New York, New York 10014, U.S.A.
Penguin Books Ltd, 27 Wrights Lane, London W8 5TZ, England
Penguin Books Australia Ltd, Ringwood, Victoria, Australia
Penguin Books Canada Ltd, 2801 John Street,
Markham, Ontario, Canada L3R 1B4
Penguin Books (N.Z.) Ltd, 182-190 Wairau Road,
Auckland 10, New Zealand

Penguin Books Ltd, Registered Offices:
Harmondsworth, Middlesex, England

First published in the United States of America by
Atheneum 1986
Published in Penguin Books 1987

3   5   7   9   10   8   6   4   2

"The Education of Mingo" was originally published in *Mother Jones*, August 1977; "Exchange Value" appeared in *Best American Short Stories 1982*, and was originally published in *Choice*, 1981; "Menagerie" was first published in *Indiana Review*, Spring 1984; "China" first appeared in *MSS*, 1983; "Alēthia" was originally published in *Antaeus #34*, June 19, 1979; "Moving Pictures" first appeared in the September 1985 issue of *North American Review*; "Popper's Disease" and "The Sorcerer's Apprentice" both appeared for the first time in *Callaloo*—in February 1982 and February 1983 respectively.

Printed in the United States of America
Set in Scotch

FOR MY FATHER

ACKNOWLEDGMENTS

Naturally, I wish to thank the sympathetic editors who first published these stories. Credit for the poem in "Alēthia" belongs to filmmaker Olivia Tappan (WGBH, Boston), who tells me she heard it long ago in a philosophy class, and I am deeply indebted to the late John Gardner for microscopically analyzing three of these stories and generally scolding me for my mistakes. Credit is also due to my wife, Joan, for just about everything I can think of, to Seattle martial-arts teacher Gray Cassidy for critiquing "China," and to Dr. Richard Hart of Long Island University for his many years of friendship and philosophical support.

CONTENTS

It is with fiction as with religion; it should present another world, and yet one to which we feel the tie.
—Herman Melville, *The Confidence Man*,
Chapter XXIII

THE EDUCATION
OF MINGO

Once, when Moses Green took his one-horse rig into town on auction day, he returned to his farm with a bondsman named Mingo. He came early in a homespun suit, stayed through the sale of fifteen slaves, and paid for Mingo in Mexican coin. A monkeylike old man, never married, with tangled hair, ginger-colored whiskers like broomstraw, and a narrow knot of a face, Moses, without children, without kinfolk, who seldom washed because he lived alone on sixty acres in southern Illinois, felt the need for a field hand and helpmate—a friend, to speak the truth plainly.

Riding home over sumps and mudholes into backcountry imprecise yet startlingly vivid in spots as though he were hurtling headlong into a rigid

New Testament parable, Moses chewed tobacco on that side of his mouth that still had good teeth and kept his eyes on the road and ears of the Appaloosa in front of his rig; he chattered mechanically to the boy, who wore tow-linen trousers a size too small, a straw hat, no shirt, and shoes repaired with wire. Moses judged him to be twenty. He was the youngest son of the reigning king of the Allmuseri, a tribe of wizards, according to the auctioneer, but they lied anyways, or so thought Moses, like abolitionists and Red Indians; in fact, for Moses Green's money nearly everybody in the New World from Anabaptists to Whigs was an outrageous liar and twisted the truth (as Moses saw it) until nothing was clear anymore. He was a dark boy. A wild, marshy-looking boy. His breastbone was broad as a barrel; he had thick hands that fell away from his wrists like weights and, on his sharp cheeks, a crescent motif. "Mingo," Moses said in a voice like gravel scrunching under a shoe, "you like rabbit? That's what I fixed for tonight. Fresh rabbit, sweet taters, and cornbread. Got hominy made from Indian corn on the fire, too. Good eatings, eh?" Then he remembered that Mingo spoke no English, and he gave the boy a friendly thump on his thigh. " 'S all right. I'm going to school you myself. Teach you everything I know, son, which ain't so joe-fired much—just common sense—but it's better'n not knowing nothing, ain't it?" Moses laughed till he shook; he liked to laugh and let his hair down

4

whenever he could. Mingo, seeing his strangely un-
filed teeth, laughed, too, but his sounded like bark-
ing. It made Moses jump a foot. He swung 'round
his head and squinted. "Reckon I'd better teach
you how to laugh, too. That half grunt, half
whinny you just made'll give a body heart failure,
son." He screwed up his lips. "You sure got a lot
to learn."

Now Moses Green was not a man for doing
things halfway. Education, as he dimly understood
it, was as serious as a heart attack. You had to have
a model, a good Christian gentleman like Moses
himself, to wash a Moor white in a single generation. As he taught Mingo farming and table eti-
quette, ciphering with knotted string, and how to
cook ashcakes, Moses constantly revised himself.
He tried not to cuss, although any mention of
Martin Van Buren or Free-Soilers made his stomach chew itself; or sop cornbread in his coffee; or
pick his nose at public market. Moses, policing all
his gestures, standing the boy behind his eyes, even
took to drinking gin from a paper sack so Mingo
couldn't see it. He felt, late at night when he looked
down at Mingo snoring loudly on his corn-shuck
mattress, now like a father, now like an artist fin-
gering something fine and noble from a rude chump
of foreign clay. It was like aiming a shotgun at the
whole world through the African, blasting away all
that Moses, according to his lights, tagged evil,
and cultivating the good; like standing, you might

say, on the sixth day, feet planted wide, trousers hitched, and remaking the world so it looked more familiar. But sometimes it scared him. He had to make sense of things for Mingo's sake. Suppose there was lightning dithering in dark clouds overhead? Did that mean rain? Or the Devil whaling his wife? Or—you couldn't waffle on a thing like that. "Rain," said Moses, solemn, scratching his neck. "For sure, it's a storm. Electri-city, Mingo." He made it a point to despoil meanings with care, chosing the ones that made the most common sense.

Slowly, Mingo got the hang of farm life, as Moses saw it—patience, grit, hard work, and prayerful silence, which wasn't easy, Moses knew, because *every*thing about him and the African was as different as night and day, even what idealistic philosophers of his time called structures of intentional consciousness (not that Moses Green called it that, being a man for whom nothing was more absolute than an ax handle, or the weight of a plow in his hands, but he knew sure enough they didn't see things quite the same way). Mingo's education, to put it plainly, involved the evaporation of one coherent, consistent, complete universe and the embracing of another one alien, contradictory, strange.

Slowly, Mingo conquered knife and spoon, then language. He picked up the old man's family name. Gradually, he learned—soaking them up like a sponge—Moses's gestures and idiosyncratic

6

body language. (Maybe too well, for Moses Green had a milk leg that needed lancing and hobbled, favoring his right knee; so did Mingo, though he was strong as an ox. His *t*'s had a reedy twang like the quiver of a ukulele string; so did Mingo's.) That African, Moses saw inside a year, was exactly the product of his own way of seeing, as much one of his products and judgments as his choice of tobacco; was, in a sense that both pleased and bumsquabbled the crusty old man, himself: a homunculus, or a distorted shadow, or—as Moses put it to his lady friend Harriet Bridgewater—his own spitting image.

"How you talk, Moses Green!" Harriet sat in a Sleepy Hollow chair on the Sunday afternoons Moses, in his one-button sack coat and Mackinaw hat, visited her after church services. She had two chins, wore a blue dress with a flounce of gauze and an apron of buff satin, above which her bosom slogged back and forth as she chattered and knitted. There were cracks in old Harriet Bridgewater's once well-stocked mind (she had been a teacher, had traveled to places Moses knew he'd never see), into which she fell during conversations, and from which she crawled with memories and facts that, Moses suspected, Harriet had spun from thin air. She was the sort of woman who, if you told her of a beautiful sunset you'd just seen, would, like as not, laugh—a squashing sound in her nose—and say, "Why, Moses, that's not beau-

7

tiful at all!" And then she'd sing a sunset more
beautiful—like the good Lord coming in a cloud—
in some faraway place like Crete or Brazil, which
you'd probably never see. That sort of woman:
haughty, worldly, so clever at times he couldn't
stand it. Why Moses Green visited her . . .

Even he didn't rightly know why. She wasn't
exactly pretty, what with her gull's nose, great
heaps of red-gold hair, and frizzy down on her
arms, but she had a certain silvery beauty intangible, elusive, inside. It was comforting after Reverend Raleigh Liverspoon's orbicular sermons to
sit a spell with Harriet in her religiously quiet,
plank-roofed common room. He put one hand in
his pocket and scratched. She knew things, that
shrewd Harriet Bridgewater, like the meaning of
Liverspoon's gnomic sermon on property, which
Moses couldn't untangle to save his life until Harriet spelled out how being and having were sorta
the same thing: "You kick a man's mule, for example, and isn't it just like ramming a boot heel in
that man's belly? Or suppose," she said, wagging a
knitting needle at him, "you don't fix those chancy
steps of yours and somebody breaks his head—his
relatives have a right to sue you into the poor-
house, Moses Green." This was said in a speech he
understood, but usually she spoke properly in a
light, musical voice, such that her language, as
Moses listened, was like song. Her dog, Ruben—a
dog so small he couldn't mount the bitches dur-

ing rutting season and, crazed, jumped Harriet's chickens instead—ran like a fleck of light around her chair. Then there was Harriet's three-decked stove, its sheet-iron stovepipe turned at a right angle, and her large wooden cupboard—all this, in comparison to his own rude, whitewashed cabin, and Harriet's endless chatter, now that her husband, Henry, was dead (when eating fish, he had breathed when he should have swallowed, then swallowed when he should have breathed), gave Moses, as he sat in his Go-to-meeting clothes nibbling egg bread (his palm under his chin to catch crumbs), a lazy feeling of warmth, well-being, and wonder. Was he sweet on Harriet Bridgewater? His mind weather-vaned—yes, no; yes, no—when he thought about it. She was awesome to him. But he didn't exactly like her opinions about his education of young Mingo. Example: "There's only *so* much he can learn, being a salt-water African and all, don't-chooknow?"

"So?"

"You know he'll never completely adjust."

"So?" he said.

"You know everything here's strange to him."

"So?" he said again.

"And it'll *always* be a little strange—like seeing the world through a fun house mirror?"

Moses knocked dottle from his churchwarden pipe, banging the bowl on the hard wooden arm of his chair until Harriet, annoyed, gave him a tight

9

look. "You oughta see him, though. I mean, he's
right smart—r'ally. It's like I just shot out another
arm and that's Mingo. Can do anything I do, like
today—he's gonna he'p Isaiah Jenson fix some
windows and watchermercallems"—he scratched
his head—"fences, over at his place." Chuckling,
Moses struck a friction match on his boot heel.
"Only thing Mingo won't do is kill chicken hawks;
he feeds 'em like they was his best friends, even
calls 'em Sir." Lightly, the old man laughed again.
He put his left ankle on his right knee and cradled
it. "But otherwise, Mingo says just what I says.
Feels what I feels."

"Well!" Harriet said with violence. Her nose
wrinkled—she rather hated his raw-smelling pipe
tobacco—and testily laid down a general principle.
"Slaves are tools with life in them, Moses, and tools
are lifeless slaves."

The old man asked, "Says who?"

"Says Aristotle." She said this arrogantly,
the way some people quote Scripture. "He owned
thirteen slaves (they were then called *banausos*),
sage Plato, fifteen, and neither felt the need to
elevate their bondsmen. The institution is old,
Moses, old, and you're asking for a peck of trouble if you keep playing God and get too close to
that wild African. If he turns turtle on you, what
then?" Quotations followed from David Hume,
who, Harriet said, once called a preposterous liar
one New World friend who informed him of a

bondsman who could play any piece on the piano after hearing it only once.

"P'raps," hemmed Moses, rocking his head. "I reckon you're right."

"I know I'm right, Moses Green." She smiled. "Harriet—"

The old woman answered, "Yes?"

"You gets me confused sometimes. Abaht my feelings. Half the time I can't rightly hear what you say, 'cause I'm all taken in by the way you say it." He struggled, shaking saliva from the stem of his pipe. "Harriet, your Henry, d'ya miss him much? I mean, abaht now you should be getting married again, don't you think? You get along okay by yourself, but I been thinking I . . . Sometimes you make me feel—"

"Yes?" She brightened. "Go on."

He didn't explain how he felt.

Moses, later on the narrow, root-covered road leading to Isaiah Jenson's cabin, thought Harriet Bridgewater wrong about Mingo and, strange to say, felt closer to the black African than to Harriet. So close, in fact, that when he pulled his rig up to Isaiah's house, he considered giving Mingo his farm when he died, God willing, as well as his knowledge, beliefs, and prejudices. Then again, maybe that was overdoing things. The boy was all Moses wanted him to be, his own emanation, but still, he thought, himself. Different enough from Moses so that he could step back and admire him.

Swinging his feet off the buckboard, he called, "Isaiah!" and, hearing no reply, hobbled, bent forward at his hips, toward the front door— "H'lo?"—which was halfway open. Why could he see no one? "Jehoshaphat!" blurted Moses. From his lower stomach a loamy feeling crawled up to his throat. "Y'all heah? Hey!" The door opened with a burst at his fingertips. Snatching off his hat, ducking his head, he stepped inside. It was dark as a poor man's pocket in there. Air within had the smell of boiled potatoes and cornbread. He saw the boy seated big as life at Isaiah's table, struggling with a big lead-colored spoon and a bowl of hominy. "You two finished al-raid-y, eh?" Moses laughed, throwing his jaw forward, full of pride, as Mingo fought mightily, his head hung over his bowl, to get food to his mouth. "Whar's that fool Isaiah?" The African pointed over his shoulder, and Moses's eyes, squinting in the weak light, followed his wagging finger to a stream of sticky black fluid like the gelatinous trail of a snail flowing from where Isaiah Jenson, cold as stone, lay crumpled next to his stove, the image of Mingo imprisoned on the retina of his eyes. Frail moonlight funneled through cracks in the roof. The whole cabin was unreal. Simply unreal. The old man's knees knocked together. His stomach jerked. Buried deep in Isaiah's forehead was a meat cleaver that exactly split his face and disconnected his features.

"Oh, my Lord!" croaked Moses. He did a little dance, half juba, half jig, on his good leg toward Isaiah, whooped, "Mingo, what'd you *do*?" Then, knowing full well what he'd done, he boxed the boy behind his ears, and shook all six feet of him until Moses's teeth, not Mingo's, rattled. The old man sat down at the table; his knees felt rubbery, and he groaned: "Lord, *Lord, Lord!*" He blew out breath, blenched, his lips skinned back over his tobacco-browned teeth, and looked square at the African. "Isaiah's daid! You understand that?"

Mingo understood that; he said so.

"And you're responsible!" He stood up, but sat down again, coughing, then pulled out his handkerchief and spit into it. "Daid! You know what daid means?" Again, he hawked and spit. "Responsible—you know what *that* means?"

He did not; he said, "Nossuh, don't know as I know that one, suh. Not Mingo, boss. No*ss*uh!"

Moses sprang up suddenly like a steel spring going off and slapped the boy till his palm stung. Briefly, the old man went bananas, pounding the boy's chest with his fists. He sat down again. Jumping up so quick made his head spin and legs wobble. Mingo protested his innocence, and it did not dawn on Moses why he seemed so indifferent until he thought back to what he'd told him about chicken hawks. Months ago, maybe five, he'd taught Mingo to kill chicken hawks and be courteous to strangers, but it got all turned around in the Afri-

can's mind (how was he to know New World cus-
toms?), so he was courteous to chicken hawks
(Moses groaned, full of gloom) and killed strangers. "You idjet!" hooted Moses. His jaw clamped
shut. He wept hoarsely for a few minutes like a
steer with the strangles. "Isaiah Jenson and me
was friends, and——" He checked himself; what'd
he said was a lie. They weren't friends at all. In
fact, he thought Isaiah Jenson was a pigheaded
fool and only tolerated the little yimp in a neigh-
borly way. Into his eye a fly bounded. Moses shook
his head wildly. He'd even sworn to Harriet, weeks
earlier, that Jenson was so troublesome, always borrowing tools and keeping them, he hoped he'd go
to Ballyhack on a red-hot rail. In his throat a knot
tightened. One of his eyelids jittered up, still itchy
from the fly; he forced it down with his finger,
then gave a slow look at the African. "Great Pe-
ter," he mumbled. "You couldn'ta known that."

"Go home now?" Mingo stretched out the stiff-
ness in his spine. "Powerful tired, boss."

Not because he wanted to go home did Moses
leave, but because he was afraid of Isaiah's body
and needed time to think things through. Dry the
air, dry the evening down the road that led them
home. As if to himself, the old man grumped, "I
gave you thought and tongue, and looka what you
done with it—they gonna catch and kill you, boy,
just as sure as I'm sitting heah."

"Mingo?" The African shook his long head,

sly; he touched his chest with one finger. "*Me*? Nossuh."

"Why the hell you keep saying that?" Moses threw his jaw forward so violently muscles in his neck stood out. "You kilt a man, and they gonna burn you crisper than an ear of corn. Ay, God, Mingo," moaned the old man, "you gotta act responsible, son!" At the thought of what they'd do to Mingo, Moses scrooched the stalk of his head into his stiff collar. He drilled his gaze at the smooth-faced African, careful not to look him in the eye, and barked, "What're you thinking *now*?"

"What Mingo know, Massa Green know. Bees like *what* Mingo sees or don't see is only what Massa Green taught him to see or don't see. Like Mingo lives through Massa Green, right?"

Moses waited, suspicious, smelling a trap. "Yeah, all that's true."

"Massa Green, he owns Mingo, right?"

"Right," snorted Moses. He rubbed the knob of his red, porous nose. "Paid good money—"

"So when Mingo works, it bees Massa Green workin', right? Bees Massa Green workin', thinkin', doin' *through* Mingo—ain't that so?"

Nobody's fool, Moses Green could latch onto a notion with no trouble at all; he turned violently off the road leading to his cabin, and plowed on toward Harriet's, pouring sweat, remembering two night visions he'd had, recurrent, where he and Mingo were wired together like say two ven-

15

triloquist's dummies, one black, one white, and there was somebody—who he didn't know, yanking their arm and leg strings simultaneously—how he couldn't figure, but he and Mingo said the same thing together until his liver-spotted hands, the knuckles tight and shriveled like old carrot skin, flew up to his face and, shrieking, he started hauling hips across a cold black countryside. But so did Mingo, *his* hands on *his* face, pumping his knees right alongside Moses, shrieking, their voice inflections identical; and then the hazy dream doorwayed luxuriously into another where he was greaved on one half of a thrip—a coin halfway between a nickel and a dime—and on the reverse side was Mingo. Shaking, Moses pulled his rig into Harriet Bridgewater's yard. His bowels, burning, felt like boiling tar. She was standing on her porch in a checkered Indian shawl, staring at them, her book still open, when Moses scrambled, tripping, skinning his knees, up her steps. He shouted, "Harriet, this boy done kilt Isaiah Jenson in cold blood." She lost color and wilted back into her doorway. Her hair was swinging in her eyes. Hands flying, he stammered in a flurry of anxiety, "But it wasn't altogether Mingo's fault—he didn't know what he was doin'."

"Isaiah? You mean Izay-yah? He didn't kill Izay-yah?"

"Yeah, aw no! Not really—" His mind stuttered to a stop.

"Whose fault is it then?" Harriet gawked at the African picking his nose in the wagon (Moses had, it's true, not policed himself as well as he'd wanted). A shiver quaked slowly up her left side. She sloughed off her confusion, and flashed, "I can tell you whose fault it is, Moses. Yours! Didn't I say not to bring that wild African here? Huh? Huh? Huh? You both should be—put to sleep."

"Aw, woman! Hesh up!" Moses threw down his hat and stomped it out of shape. "You just all upsetted." Truth to tell, he was not the portrait of composure himself. There were rims of dirt in his nails. His trouser legs had blood splattered on them. Moses stamped his feet to shake road powder off his boots. "You got any spirits in the house? I need your he'p to untangle this thing, but I ain't hardly touched a drop since I bought Mingo, and my throat's pretty dr—"

"You'll just have to get it yourself—on the top shelf of the cupboard." She touched her face, fingers spread, with a dazed gesture. There was suddenly in her features the intensity found in the look of people who have a year, a month, a minute only to live. "I think I'd better sit down." Lowering herself onto her rocker, she cradled on her lap a volume by one M. Shelley, a recent tale of monstrosity and existential horror, then she demurely settled her breasts. "It's just like you, Moses Green, to bring all your bewilderments to me."

The old man's face splashed into a huge,

foamy smile. He kissed her gently on both eyes, and Harriet, in return, rubbed her cheek like a cat against his gristly jaw. Moses felt lighter than a feather. "Got to have somebody, don't I?"

In the common room, Moses rifled through the cupboard, came up with a bottle of luke-warm bourbon and, hands trembling, poured himself three fingers' worth in a glass. Then, because he figured he deserved it, he refilled his glass and, draining it slowly, sloshing it around in his mouth, considered his options. He could turn Mingo over to the law and let it go at that, but damned if he couldn't shake loose the idea that killing the boy somehow wouldn't put things to rights; it would be like they were killing Moses himself, destroying a part of his soul. Besides, whatever the African'd done, it was what he'd learned through Moses, who was not the most reliable lens for looking at things. You couldn't rightly call a man responsible if, in some utterly alien place, he was without power, without privilege, without property—was, in fact, property—if he had no position, had nothing, or virtually next to nothing, and nothing was his product or judgment. "Be damned!" Moses spit. It was a bitter thing to siphon your being from someone else. He knew that now. It was like, on another level, what Liverspoon had once tried to deny about God and man: *If* God was (and now Moses wasn't all that sure), and *if* He made the

world, then a man didn't have to answer for anything. Rape or murder, it all referred back to
who-or-whatever was responsible for that world's
make-up. Chest fallen, he tossed away his glass,
lifted the bottle to his lips, then nervously lit his
pipe. Maybe . . . maybe they could run, if it came
to that, and start all over again in Missouri, where
he'd teach Mingo the difference between chicken
hawks and strangers. But, sure as day, he'd do it
again. He couldn't change. What was *was*. They'd
be running forever, across all space, all time—so
he imagined—like fugitives with no fingers, no
toes, like two thieves or yokefellows, each with some
God-awful secret that could annihilate the other.
Naw! Moses thought. His blood beat up. The deep,
powerful stroke of his heart made him wince. His
tobacco maybe. Too strong. He sent more whiskey
crashing down his throat. *Naw!* You couldn't have
nothing and just go as you pleased. How strange
that owner and owned magically dissolved into each
other like two crossing shafts of light (or, if he'd
known this, which he did not, particles, subatomic,
interconnected in a complex skein of relatedness).
Shoot him maybe, reabsorb Mingo, was that more
merciful? *Naw!* He was fast; fast. Then manumit
the African? Noble gesture, that. But how in blazes
could he disengage himself when Mingo shored up,
sustained, *let be* Moses's world with all its sores and
blemishes every time he opened his oily black eyes?

Thanks to the trouble he took cementing Mingo to his own mind, he could not, by thunder, do without him now. Giving him his freedom, handing it to him like a rasher of bacon, would shackle Mingo to him even more. There seemed, just then, no solution.

Undecided, but mercifully drunk now, his pipebowl too hot to hold any longer, Moses, who could not speak his mind to Harriet Bridgewater unless he'd tied one on, called out: "I come to a decision. Not about Mingo, but you'n' me." It was then seven o'clock. He shambled, feet shuffling, toward the door. "Y'know, I was gonna ask you to marry me this morning"—he laughed; whiskey made his scalp tingle—"but I figured living alone was better when I thoughta how married folks—and sometimes wimmin with dogs—got to favoring each other . . . like they was wax candles flowing tergether. Hee-hee." He stepped gingerly, holding the bottle high, his ears brick red, face streaky from wind-dried sweat, back onto the quiet porch. He heard a moan. It was distinctly a moan. "Harriet? Harriet, I ain't put it too well, but I'm asking you now." On the porch her rocker slid back, forth, squeaking on the floorboards. Moses's bottle fell—*bip!*—down the stairs, bounced out into the yard, rolled, and bumped into Harriet Bridgewater. Naw, he thought. Aw, naw. By the wagon, by a chopping block near a pile of split faggots, by the ruin of an old handpump caked with rust, she lay on her side, the back fastenings of her dress

20

burst open, her mouth a perfect O. The sight so wounded him he wept like a child. It was then seven-fifteen.

October 7 of the year of grace 1855.

Midnight found Moses Green still staring down at her. He felt sick and crippled and dead inside. Every shadowed object thinging in the yard beyond, wrenched up from its roots, hazed like shapes in a hallucination, was a sermon on vanity; every time he moved his eyes he stared into a grim homily on the deadly upas of race and relatedness. Now he had no place to stand. Now he was undone. "Mingo . . . come ovah heah." He was very quiet.

"Suh?" The lanky African jumped down from the wagon, faintly innocent, faintly diabolical. Removed from the setting of Moses's farm, the boy looked strangely elemental; his skin had the texture of plant life, the stones of his eyes an odd, glossy quality like those of a spider, which cannot be read. "Talky old hen daid now, boss."

The old man's face shattered. "I was gonna marry that woman!"

"Naw." Mingo frowned. From out of his frown a huge grin flowered. "You say—I'm quoting you now, suh—a man needs a quiet, patient, uncomplaining woman, right?"

Moses croaked, "When did I say that?"

"Yesstiday." Mingo yawned. He looked sleepy. "Go home now, boss?"

"Not just yet." Moses Green, making an ef-

fort to pull himself to his full height, failed. "You
lie face down—heah me?—with your hands ovah
your head till I come back." With Mingo hugging
the front steps, Moses took the stairs back inside,
found the flintlock Harriet kept in her cupboard
on account of slaves who swore to die in the skin
of freemen, primed it, and stepped back, so slowly,
to the yard. Outside, the air seemed thinner. Bend-
ing forward, perspiring at his upper lip, Moses
tucked the cold barrel into the back of Mingo's
neck, cushioning it in a small socket of flesh above
the African's broad shoulders. With his thumb he
pulled the hammer back. Springs in the flintlock
whined. Deep inside his throat, as if he were speaking through his stomach, he talked to the dark poll
of the boy's back-slanting head.

"You ain't never gonna understand why I
gotta do this. You a saddle across my neck, always
will be, even though it ain't rightly all your fault.
Mingo, you more me than I am myself. Me planed
away to the bone! Ya understand?" He coughed
and went on miserably: "All the wrong, all the good
you do, now or tomorrow—it's me indirectly doing
it, but without the lies and excuses, without the
feeling what's its foundation, with all the polite
make-up and apologies removed. It's an empty gesture, like the swing of a shadow's arm. You can't
never see things exactly the way I do. I'm guilty.
It was me set the gears in motion. Me . . ." Away
in the octopoid darkness a wild bird—a night-

hawk maybe—screeched. It shot noisily away with blurred wings askirring when the sound of hoofs and wagons rumbled closer. Eyes narrowed to slits, Moses said—a dry whisper—"Get up, you damned fool." He let his round shoulders slump. Mingo let his broad shoulders slump. "Take the horses," Moses said; he pulled himself up to his rig, then sat, his knees together beside the boy. Mingo's knees drew together. Moses's voice changed. It began to rasp and wheeze; so did Mingo's. "Missouri," said the old man, not to Mingo but to the dusty floor of the buckboard, "if I don't misremember, is off thataway somewheres in the west."

EXCHANGE VALUE

Me and my brother, Loftis, came in by the old lady's window. There was some kinda boobytrap—boxes of broken glass—that shoulda warned us Miss Bailey wasn't the easy mark we made her to be. She been living alone for twenty years in 4-B down the hall from Loftis and me, long before our folks died—a hincty, halfbald West Indian woman with a craglike face, who kept her door barricaded, shutters closed, and wore the same sorry-looking outfit—black wingtip shoes, cropfingered gloves in winter, and a man's floppy hat—like maybe she dressed half-asleep or in a dark attic. Loftis, he figured Miss Bailey had some grandtheft dough stashed inside, jim, or leastways a shoebox full of money, 'cause she never spent a nickel on herself,

27

not even for food, and only left her place at night.

Anyway, we figured Miss Bailey was gone. Her mailbox be full, and Pookie White, who run the Thirty-ninth Street Creole restaurant, he say she ain't dropped by in days to collect the handouts he give her so she can get by. So here's me and Loftis, tipping around Miss Bailey's blackdark kitchen. The floor be littered with fruitrinds, roaches, old food furred with blue mold. Her dirty dishes be stacked in a sink feathered with cracks, and it looks like the old lady been living, lately, on Ritz crackers and Department of Agriculture (Welfare Office) peanut butter. Her toilet be stopped up, too, and, on the bathroom floor, there's five Maxwell House coffee cans full of shit. Me, I was closing her bathroom door when I whiffed this evil smell so bad, so thick, I could hardly breathe, and what air I breathed was stifling, like solid fluid in my throatpipes, like broth or soup. "Cooter," Loftis whisper, low, across the room, "you smell that?" He went right on sniffing it, like people do for some reason when something be smelling stanky, then took out his headrag and held it over his mouth. "Smells like something crawled up in here and died!" Then, head low, he slipped his long self into the living room. Me, I stayed by the window, gulping for air, and do you know why?

You oughta know, up front, that I ain't too good at this gangster stuff, and I had a real bad feeling about Miss Bailey from the get-go. Mama used to say it was Loftis, not me, who'd go places— I see her standing at the sideboard by the sink now, big as a Frigidaire, white flour to her elbows, a washtowel over her shoulder, while we ate a breakfast of cornbread and syrup. Loftis, he graduated fifth at DuSable High School, had two gigs and, like Papa, he be always wanting the things white people had out in Hyde Park, where Mama did daywork sometimes. Loftis, he be the kind of brother who buys *Esquire*, sews Hart, Schaffner & Marx labels in Robert Hall suits, talks properlike, packs his hair with Murray's; and he took classes in politics and stuff at the Black People's Topographical Library in the late 1960s. At thirty, he make his bed military-style, reads *Black Scholar* on the bus he takes to the plant, and, come hell or high water, plans to make a Big Score. Loftis, he say I'm 'bout as useful on a hustle—or when it comes to getting ahead—as a headcold, and he says he has to count my legs sometimes to make sure I ain't a mule, seeing how, for all my eighteen years, I can't keep no job and sorta stay close to home, watching TV, or reading *World's Finest* comic books, or maybe just laying dead, listening to music, imagining I see faces or foreign places in water stains on the wallpaper, 'cause some days, when I remember Papa, then Mama, killing theyselves for chump change—a pitiful li'l bowl of porridge—I get to thinking that even if I ain't had all I wanted, maybe I've had, you know, all I'm ever gonna get.

"Cooter," Loftis say from the living room. "You best get in here quick."

Loftis, he'd switched on Miss Bailey's bright, overhead living room lights, so for a second I couldn't see and started coughing—the smell be so powerful it hit my nostrils like coke—and when my eyes cleared, shapes come forward in the light, and I thought for an instant like I'd slipped in space. I seen why Loftis called me, and went back two steps. See, 4-B's so small if you ring Miss Bailey's doorbell, the toilet'd flush. But her living room, webbed in dust, be filled to the max with dollars of all denominations, stacks of stock in General Motors, Gulf Oil, and 3M Company in old White Owl cigar boxes, battered purses, or bound in pink rubber bands. It be like the kind of cubbyhole kids play in, but filled with . . . *things*: everything, like a world inside the world, you take it from me, so like picturebook scenes of plentifulness you could seal yourself off in here and settle forever. Loftis and me both drew breath suddenly. There be unopened cases of Jack Daniel's, three safes cemented to the floor, hundreds of matchbooks, unworn clothes, a fuel-burning stove, dozens of wedding rings, rubbish, World War II magazines, a carton of a hundred canned sardines, mink stoles, old rags, a birdcage, a bucket of silver dollars, thousands of books, paintings, quarters in tobacco cans, two pianos, glass jars of pennies, a set of bagpipes, an almost complete Model A Ford dappled with rust, and, I swear, three sections of a dead tree.

"Damn!" My head be light; I sat on an upended peach crate and picked up a bottle of Jack Daniel's.

"Don't you touch *any*thing!" Loftis, he panting a little; he slap both hands on a table. "Not until we inventory this stuff."

"Inventory? Aw, Lord, Loftis," I say, "something ain't *right* about this stash. There could be a curse on it. . . ."

"Boy, sometime you act weak-minded."

"For real, Loftis, I got a feeling. . . ."

Loftis, he shucked off his shoes, and sat down heavily on the lumpy arm of a stuffed chair. "Don't say *any*thing." He chewed his knuckles, and for the first time Loftis looked like he didn't know his next move. "Let me think, okay?" He squeezed his nose in a way he has when thinking hard, sighed, then stood up and say, "There's something you better see in that bedroom yonder. Cover up your mouth."

"Loftis, I ain't going in there."

He look at me right funny then. "She's a miser, that's all. She saves things."

"But a tree?" I say. "Loftis, a *tree* ain't normal!"

"Cooter, I ain't gonna tell you twice."

Like always, I followed Loftis, who swung his flashlight from the plant—he a night watchman—into Miss Bailey's bedroom, but me, I'm thinking how trippy this thing is getting, remembering how, last year, when I had a paper route, the old lady, with her queer, crablike walk, pulled my coat for some change in the hallway, and when I give her a handful of dimes, she say, like one of them spooks on old-time radio, "Thank you, Co-o-oter," then gulped the coins down like aspirin, no lie, and scurried off like a hunchback. Me, I wanted no parts of this squirrely old broad, but Loftis, he holding my wrist now, beaming his light onto a low bed. The room had a funny, museumlike smell. Real sour. It was full of dirty laundry. And I be sure the old lady's stuff had a terrible string attached when Loftis, looking away, lifted her bedsheets and a knot of black flies rose. I stepped back and held my breath. Miss Bailey be in her long-sleeved flannel nightgown, bloated, like she'd been blown up by a bicycle pump, her old face caved in with rot, flyblown, her fingers big and colored like spoiled bananas. Her wristwatch be ticking softly beside a half-eaten hamburger. Above the bed, her wall had roaches squashed in little swirls of bloodstain. Maggots clustered in her eyes, her ears, and one fist-sized rat hissed inside her flesh. My eyes snapped shut. My knees failed; then I did a Hollywood faint. When I surfaced, Loftis, he be sitting beside me in the living room, where he'd drug me, reading a wrinkled, yellow article from the *Chicago Daily Defender*.

"Listen to this," Loftis say. " 'Elnora Bailey, forty-five, a Negro housemaid in the Highland Park home of Henry Conners, is the beneficiary of her employer's will. An old American family, the Conners arrived in this country on the *Providence* shortly after the voyage of the *Mayflower*. The family flourished in the early days of the 1900s.'. . ." He went on, getting breath: " 'A distinguished and wealthy industrialist, without heirs or a wife, Conners willed his entire estate to Miss Bailey of 3347 North Clark Street for her twenty years of service to his family.'. . ." Loftis, he give that Geoffrey Holder laugh of his, low and deep; then it eased up his throat until it hit a high note and tipped his head back onto his shoulders. "Cooter, that was before we was born! Miss Bailey kept this in the Bible next to her bed."

Standing, I braced myself with one hand against the wall. "She didn't earn it?"

"Naw." Loftis, he folded the paper—"Not one penny"—and stuffed it in his shirt pocket. His jaw looked tight as a horseshoe. "Way *I* see it," he say, "this was her one shot in a lifetime to be rich, but being country, she had backward ways and blew it." Rubbing his hands, he stood up to survey the living room. "Somebody's gonna find Miss Bailey soon, but if we stay on the case—

Cooter, don't square up on me now—we can tote everything to our place before daybreak. Best we start with the big stuff."

"But why didn't she *use* it, huh? Tell me that?"

Loftis, he don't pay me no mind. When he gets an idea in his head, you can't dig it out with a chisel. How long it took me and Loftis to inventory, then haul Miss Bailey's queer old stuff to our crib, I can't say, but that cranky old ninnyhammer's hoard come to $879,543 in cash money, thirty-two bank books (some deposits be only $5), and me, I wasn't sure I was dreaming or what, but I suddenly flashed on this feeling, once we left her flat, that all the fears Loftis and me had about the future be gone, 'cause Miss Bailey's property was the past—the power of that fellah Henry Conners trapped like a bottle spirit—which we could live off, so it was the future, too, pure potential: can *do*. Loftis got to talking on about how that piano we pushed home be equal to a thousand bills, jim, which equals, say, a bad TEAC A-3340 tape deck, or a down payment on a deuce-and-a-quarter. Its value be (Loftis say) that of a universal standard of measure, relational, unreal as number, so that tape deck could turn, magically, into two gold lamé suits, a trip to Tijuana, or twenty-five blow jobs from a ho—we had $879,543 worth of wishes, if you can deal with that. Be like Miss Bailey's stuff is raw energy, and Loftis and me, like wizards, could transform her stuff into anything else at will. All we had to do, it seemed to me, was decide exactly what to exchange it for.

While Loftis studied this over (he looked funny, like a potato trying to say something, after the inventory, and sat, real quiet, in the kitchen), I filled my pockets with fifties, grabbed me a cab downtown to grease, yum, at one of them high-hat restaurants in the Loop. . . . But then I thought better of it, you know, like I'd be out of place—just another jig putting on airs—and scarfed instead at a ribjoint till both my eyes bubbled. This fat lady making fishburgers in the back favored an old hardleg baby-sitter I once had, a Mrs. Paine who made me eat ocher, and I wanted so bad to say, "Loftis and me Got Ovuh," but I couldn't put that in the wind, could I, so I hatted up. Then I copped a boss silk necktie, cashmere socks, and a whistle-slick maxi leather jacket on State Street, took cabs *every*where, but when I got home that evening, a funny, Pandora-like feeling hit me. I took off the jacket, boxed it—it looked trifling in the hallway's weak light—and, tired, turned my key in the door. I couldn't get in. Loftis, he'd changed the lock and, when he finally let me in, looking vaguer, crabby, like something out of the Book of Revelations, I seen this elaborate, booby-trapped tunnel of cardboard and razor blades behind him, with a two-foot space just big enough for him or me to crawl through. That wasn't all.

Two bags of trash from the furnace room downstairs be sitting inside the door. Loftis, he give my leather jacket this evil look, hauled me inside, and hit me upside my head.

"How much this thing set us back?"

"Two fifty." My jaws got tight; I toss him my receipt. "You want me to take it back? Maybe I can get something else. . . ."

Loftis, he say, not to me, but to the receipt, "Remember the time Mama give me that ring we had in the family for fifty years? And I took it to Merchandise Mart and sold it for a few pieces of candy?" He hitched his chair forward and sat with his elbows on his knees. "That's what you did, Cooter. You crawled into a Clark bar." He commence to rip up my receipt, then picked up his flashlight and keys. "As soon as you buy something you *lose* the power to buy something." He button up his coat with holes in the elbows, showing his blue shirt, then turned 'round at the tunnel to say, "Don't touch Miss Bailey's money, or drink her splo, or do *any*thing until I get back."

"Where you going?"

"To work. It's Wednesday, ain't it?"

"You going to work?"

"Yeah."

"You got to go *really*? Loftis," I say, "what you brang them bags of trash in here for?"

"It ain't trash!" He cut his eyes at me. "There's good clothes in there. Mr. Peterson tossed

36

them out, he don't care, but I saw some use in them, that's all."

"Loftis . . ."

"Yeah?"

"What we gonna do with all this money?"

Loftis pressed his fingers to his eyelids, and for a second he looked caged, or like somebody'd kicked him in his stomach. Then he cut me some slack: "Let me think on it tonight—it don't pay to rush—then we can TCB, okay?"

Five hours after Loftis leave for work, that old blister Mr. Peterson, our landlord, he come collecting rent, find Mrs. Bailey's body in apartment 4-B, and phoned the fire department. Me, I be folding my new jacket in tissue paper to keep it fresh, adding the box to Miss Bailey's unsunned treasures when two paramedics squeezed her on a long stretcher through a crowd in the hallway. See, I had to pin her from the stairhead, looking down one last time at this dizzy old lady, and I seen something in her face, like maybe she'd been poor as Job's turkey for thirty years, suffering that special Negro fear of using up what little we get in this life—Loftis, he call that entropy—believing in her belly, and for all her faith, jim, that there just ain't no more coming tomorrow from grace, or the Lord, or from her own labor, like she can't kill nothing, and won't nothing die . . . so when Conners will her his wealth, it put her through changes, she be spellbound, possessed by the promise of life, panicky about depletion, and locked now in the past 'cause *every* purchase, you know, has to be a poor buy: a loss of life. Me, I wasn't worried none. Loftis, he got a brain trained by years of talking trash with people in Frog Hudson's barbershop on Thirty-fifth Street. By morning, I knew, he'd have some kinda wheeze worked out.

But Loftis, he don't come home. Me, I got kinda worried. I listen to the hi-fi all day Thursday, only pawing outside to peep down the stairs, like that'd make Loftis come sooner. So Thursday go by; and come Friday the head's out of kilter— first there's an ogrelike belch from the toilet bowl, then water bursts from the bathroom into the kitchen—and me, I can't call the super (How do I explain the tunnel?), so I gave up and quit bailing. But on Saturday, I could smell greens cooking next door. Twice I almost opened Miss Bailey's sardines, even though starving be less an evil than eating up our stash, but I waited till it was dark and, with my stomach talking to me, stepped outside to Pookie White's, lay a hard-luck story on him, and Pookie, he give me some jambalaya and gumbo. Back home in the living room, finger-feeding myself, barricaded in by all that hope-made material, the Kid felt like a king in his counting room, and I copped some Zs in an armchair till I heard the door move on its hinges, then bumping in the tunnel, and a heavy-footed walk thumped into the bedroom.

"Loftis?" I rubbed my eyes. "You back?" It be Sunday morning. Six-thirty sharp. Darkness dissolved slowly into the strangeness of twilight, with the rays of sunlight surging at exactly the same angle they fall each evening, as if the hour be an island, a moment outside time. Me, I'm afraid Loftis gonna fuss 'bout my not straightening up, letting things go. I went into the bathroom, poured water in the one-spigot washstand—brown rust come bursting out in flakes—and rinsed my face. "Loftis, you supposed to be home four days ago. Hey," I say, toweling my face, "you okay?" How come he don't answer me? Wiping my hands on the seat on my trousers, I tipped into Loftis's room. He sleeping with his mouth open. His legs be drawn up, both fists clenched between his knees. He'd kicked his blanket on the floor. In his sleep, Loftis laughed, or moaned, it be hard to tell. His eyelids, not quite shut, show slits of white. I decided to wait till Loftis wake up for his decision, but turning, I seen his watch, keys, and what looked in the first stain of sunlight to be a carefully wrapped piece of newspaper on his nightstand. The sunlight swelled to a bright shimmer, focusing the bedroom slowly like solution do a photographic image in the developer. And then something so freakish went down I ain't sure it took place. Fumble-fingered, I unfolded the paper, and inside be a blemished penny. It be like suddenly somebody slapped my head from behind. Taped on the penny be a slip of paper, and on the paper be the note "Found while walking down Devon Avenue." I hear Loftis mumble like he trapped in a nightmare. "Hold tight," I whisper. "It's all right." Me, I wanted to tell Loftis how Miss Bailey looked four days ago, that maybe it didn't have to be like that for us—did it?—because we could change. Couldn't we? Me, I pull his packed sheets over him, wrap up the penny, and, when I locate Miss Bailey's glass jar in the living room, put it away carefully, for now, with the rest of our things.

MENAGERIE,
A CHILD'S FABLE

Among watchdogs in Seattle, Berkeley was known generally as one of the best. Not the smartest, but steady. A pious German shepherd (Black Forest origins, probably), with big shoulders, black gums, and weighing more than some men, he sat guard inside the glass door of Tilford's Pet Shoppe, watching the pedestrians scurry along First Avenue, wondering at the derelicts who slept ever so often inside the foyer at night, and sometimes he nodded when things were quiet in the cages behind him, lulled by the bubbling of the fishtanks, dreaming of an especially fine meal he'd once had, or the little female poodle, a real flirt, owned by the aerobic dance teacher (who was no saint herself) a few doors down the street; but Berkeley was, for all his woolgathering, never asleep at the switch. He took his work seriously. Moreover, he knew exactly where he was at every moment, what he was doing, and why he was doing it, which was more than can be said for most people, like Mr. Tilford, a real gumboil, whose ways were mysterious to Berkeley. Sometimes he treated the animals cruelly, or taunted them; he saw them not as pets but profit. Nevertheless, no vandals, or thieves, had ever brought trouble through the doors or windows of Tilford's Pet Shoppe, and Berkeley, confident of his power but never flaunting it, faithful to his master though he didn't deserve it, was certain that none ever would.

At closing time, Mr. Tilford, who lived alone, as most cruel men do, always checked the cages, left a beggarly pinch of food for all the animals, and a single biscuit for Berkeley. The watchdog always hoped for a pat on his head, or for Tilford to play with him, some sign of approval to let him know he was appreciated, but such as this never came. Mr. Tilford had thick glasses and a thin voice, was stubborn, hot-tempered, a drunkard and a loner who, sliding toward senility, sometimes put his shoes in the refrigerator, and once—Berkeley winced at the memory—put a Persian he couldn't sell in the Mix Master during one of his binges. Mainly, the owner drank and watched television, which was something else Berkeley couldn't understand. More than once he'd mistaken gunfire on

44

screen for the real thing (a natural error, since no one told him violence was entertainment for some), howled loud enough to bring down the house, and Tilford booted him outside. Soon enough, Berkeley stopped looking for approval; he didn't bother to get up from biting fleas behind the counter when he heard the door slam.

But it seemed one night too early for closing time. His instincts on this had never been wrong before. He trotted back to the darkened storeroom; then his mouth snapped shut. His feeding bowl was as empty as he'd last left it.

"Say, Berkeley," said Monkey, whose cage was near the storeroom. "What's goin' on? Tilford didn't put out the food."

Berkeley didn't care a whole lot for Monkey, and usually he ignored him. He was downright wicked, a comedian always grabbing his groin to get a laugh, throwing feces, or fooling with the other animals, a clown who'd do anything to crack up the iguana, Frog, Parrot, and the Siamese, even if it meant aping Mr. Tilford, which he did well, though Berkeley found this parody frightening, like playing with fire, or literally biting the hand that fed you. But he, too, was puzzled by Tilford's abrupt departure.

"I don't know," said Berkeley. "He'll be back, I guess."

Monkey, his head through his cage, held onto the bars like a movie inmate. "Wanna bet?"

"What're you talking about?"

"Wake *up*," said Monkey. "Tilford's sick. I seen better faces on dead guppies in the fishtank. You ever see a pulmonary embolus?" Monkey ballooned his cheeks, then started breathing hard enough to hyperventilate, rolled up both red-webbed eyes, then crashed back into his cage, howling.

Not thinking this funny at all, Berkeley padded over to the front door, gave Monkey a grim look, then curled up against the bottom rail, waiting for Tilford's car to appear. Cars of many kinds, and cars of different sizes, came and went, but that Saturday night the owner did not show. Nor the next morning, or the following night, and on the second day it was not only Monkey but every beast, bird, and fowl in the Shoppe that shook its cage or tank and howled at Berkeley for an explanation—an ear-shattering babble of tongues, squawks, trills, howls, mewling, bellows, hoots, blorting, and belly growls because Tilford had collected everything from baby alligators to zebra-striped fish, an entire federation of cultures, with each animal having its own distinct, inviolable nature (so they said), the rows and rows of counters screaming with a plurality of so many backgrounds, needs, and viewpoints that Berkeley, his head splitting, could hardly hear his own voice above the din.

"Be patient!" he said. "Believe me, he's comin' back!"

"Come *off* it," said one of three snakes. "Monkey says Tilford's *dead*. Question is, what're we gonna *do* about it?"

Berkeley looked, witheringly, toward the front door. His empty stomach gurgled like a sewer. It took a tremendous effort to untangle his thoughts. "If we can just hold on a—"

"We're *hungry*!" shouted Frog. "We'll starve before old Tilford comes back!"

Throughout this turmoil, the shouting, beating of wings, which blew feathers everywhere like confetti, and an angry slapping of fins that splashed water to the floor, Monkey simply sat quietly, taking it all in, stroking his chin as a scholar might. He waited for a space in the shouting, then pushed his head through the cage again. His voice was calm, studied, like an old-time barrister before the bar. "Berkeley? Don't get mad now, but I think it's obvious that there's only one solution."

"What?"

"Let us out," said Monkey. "Open the cages."

"No!"

"We've got a crisis situation here." Monkey sighed like one of the elderly, tired lizards, as if his solution bothered even him. "It calls for courage, radical decisions. You're in charge until Tilford gets back. That means you gotta feed us, but you can't do that, can you? Only one here with hands is *me*. See, we all have different talents, unique gifts. If you let us out, we can pool our resources. I can *open* the feed bags!"

"You can?" The watchdog swallowed.

"Uh-huh." He wiggled his fingers dexterously, then the digits on his feet. "But somebody's gotta throw the switch on this cage. I can't reach it. Dog, I'm asking you to be democratic! Keeping us locked up is fascist!"

The animals clamored for release; they took up Monkey's cry, "Self-determination!" But everything within Berkeley resisted this idea, the possibility of chaos it promised, so many different, quarrelsome creatures uncaged, set loose in a low-ceilinged Shoppe where even he had trouble finding room to turn around between the counters, pens, displays of paraphernalia, and heavy, bubbling fishtanks. The chances for mischief were incalculable, no question of that, but slow starvation was certain if he didn't let them in the storeroom. Furthermore, he didn't want to be called a fascist. It didn't seem fair, Monkey saying that, making him look bad in front of the others. It was the one charge you couldn't defend yourself against. Against his better judgment, the watchdog rose on his hindlegs and, praying this was the right thing, forced open the cage with his teeth. For a moment Monkey did not move. He drew breath loudly and stared at the open door. Cautiously, he stepped out, stood up to his full height, rubbed his bony hands together, then did a little dance and began throwing open the other cages one by one.

Berkeley cringed. "The tarantula, too?"

Monkey gave him a cold glance over one shoulder. "You should get to know him, Berkeley. Don't be a bigot."

Berkeley shrank back as Tarantula, an item ordered by a Hell's Angel who never claimed him, shambled out—not so much an insect, it seemed to Berkeley, as Pestilence on legs. ("Be fair!" he scolded himself. "He's okay, I'm okay, we're all okay.") He watched helplessly as Monkey smashed the ant farm, freed the birds, and then the entire troupe, united by the spirit of a bright, common future, slithered, hopped, crawled, bounded, flew, and clawed its way into the storeroom to feed. All except crankled, old Tortoise, whom Monkey hadn't freed, who, in fact, didn't want to be released and snapped at Monkey's fingers when he tried to open his cage. No one questioned it. Tortoise had escaped the year before, remaining at large for a week, and then he returned mysteriously on his own, his eyes strangely unfocused, as if he'd seen the end of the world, or a vision of the world to come. He hadn't spoken in a year. Hunched inside his shell, hardly eating at all, Tortoise lived in the Shoppe, but you could hardly say he was part of it, and even the watchdog was a little leery of him.

Berkeley, for his part, had lost his hunger. He dragged himself, wearily, to the front door, barked frantically when a woman walked by, hoping she would stop, but after seeing the window sign, which read—CLOSED—from his side, she stepped briskly on. His tail between his legs, he went slowly back to the storeroom, hoping for the best, but what he found there was no sight for a peace-loving watchdog.

True to his word, Monkey had broken open the feed bags and boxes of food, but the animals, who had always been kept apart by Tilford, discovered as they crowded into the tiny storeroom and fell to eating that sitting down to table with creatures so different in their gastronomic inclinations took the edge off their appetites. The birds found the eating habits of the reptiles, who thought eggs were a delicacy, disgusting and drew away in horror; the reptiles, who were proud of being cold-blooded, and had an elaborate theory of beauty based on the aesthetics of scales, thought the body heat of the mammals cloying and nauseating, and refused to feed beside them, and this was fine for the mammals, who, led by Monkey, distrusted any-one odd enough to be born in an egg, and dismissed them as lowlifes on the evolutionary scale; they were shoveling down everything—bird food, dog biscuits, and even the thin wafers reserved for the fish.

"Don't touch that!" said Berkeley. "The fish have to eat, too! They can't leave the tanks!"

Monkey, startled by the watchdog, looked at the wafers in his fist thoughtfully for a second, then crammed them into his mouth. "That's their problem."

Deep inside, Berkeley began a rumbling bark, let it build slowly, and by the time it hit the air it was a full-throated growl so frightening that Monkey jumped four, maybe five feet into the air. He threw the wafers at Berkeley. "Okay—okay, give it to 'em! But remember one thing, dog: You're a mammal, too. It's unnatural to take sides against your own kind."

Scornfully, the watchdog turned away, trembling with fury. He snuffled up the wafers in his mouth, carried them to the huge, man-sized tanks, and dropped them in amongst the sea horses, guppies, and jellyfish throbbing like hearts. Goldfish floated toward him, his voice and fins fluttering. He kept a slightly startled expression. "What the hell is going on? Where's Mr. Tilford?"

Berkeley strained to keep his voice steady. "Gone."

"For good?" asked Goldfish. "Berkeley, we heard what the others said. They'll let us starve—"

"No," he said. "I'll protect you."

Goldfish bubbled relief, then looked panicky again. "What if Tilford doesn't come back ever?"

The watchdog let his head hang. The thought seemed too terrible to consider. He said, more to console himself than Goldfish, "It's his Shoppe. He has to come back."

"But suppose he *is* dead, like Monkey says." Goldfish's unblinking, lidless eyes grabbed at Berkeley and refused to release his gaze. "Then it's our Shoppe, right?"

"Eat your dinner."

Goldfish called, "Berkeley, wait—"

But the watchdog was deeply worried now. He returned miserably to the front door. He let fly a long, plaintive howl, his head tilted back like a mountaintop wolf silhouetted by the moon in a Warner Brothers cartoon—he did look like that— his insides hurting with the thought that if Tilford was dead, or indifferent to their problems, that if no one came to rescue them, then they were dead, too. True, there was a great deal of Tilford inside Berkeley, what he remembered from his training as a pup, but this faint sense of procedure and fair play hardly seemed enough to keep order in the Shoppe, maintain the peace, and more important provide for them as the old man had. He'd never looked upon himself as a leader, preferring to attribute his distaste for decision to a rare ability to see all sides. He was no hero like Old Yeller, or the legendary Gellert, and testing his ribs with his teeth, he wondered how much weight he'd lost from worry. Ten pounds? Twenty pounds? He covered both eyes with his black paws, whimpered a little, feeling a failure of nerve, a soft white core of fear like a slug in his stomach. Then he drew breath and, with it, new determination. The owner couldn't be dead. Monkey would never convince him of that. He simply had business elsewhere. And when he returned, he would expect to find the Shoppe as he left it. Maybe even running more smoothly, like an old Swiss watch that he had wound and left ticking. When the watchdog tightened his jaws, they creaked at the hinges, but he tightened them all the same. His eyes narrowed. No evil had visited the Shoppe from outside. He'd seen to that. None, he vowed, would destroy it from within.

But he could not be everywhere at once. The corrosion grew day by day. Cracks, then fissures began to appear, it seemed to Berkeley, everywhere, and in places where he least expected them. Puddles and pyramidal plops were scattered underfoot like traps. Bacterial flies were everywhere. Then came maggots. Hamsters gnawed at electrical cords in the storeroom. Frog fell sick with a genital infection. The fish, though the gentlest of creatures, caused undertow by demanding day-and-night protection, claiming they were handicapped in the competition for food, confined to their tanks, and besides, they were from the most ancient tree; all life came from the sea, they argued, the others owed *them*.

Old blood feuds between beasts erupted, too,

grudges so tired you'd have thought them long buried, but not so. The Siamese began to give Berkeley funny looks, and left the room whenever he entered. Berkeley let him be, thinking he'd come to his senses. Instead, he jumped Rabbit when Berkeley wasn't looking, the product of this assault promising a new creature—a cabbit—with jack-rabbit legs and long feline whiskers never seen in the Pet Shoppe before. Rabbit took this badly. In the beginning she sniffed a great deal, and with good reason—rape was a vicious thing—but her grief and pain got out of hand, and soon she was lost in it with no way out, like a child in a dark forest, and began organizing the females of every species to stop cohabiting with the males. Berkeley stood back, afraid to butt in because Rabbit said that it was none of his damned business and he was as bad as all the rest. He pleaded reason, his eyes burnt-out from sleeplessness, with puffy bags beneath them, and when that did no good, he pleaded restraint.

"The storeroom's half-empty," he told Monkey on the fifth day. "If we don't start rationing the food, we'll starve."

"There's always food."

Berkeley didn't like the sound of that. "Where?"

Smiling, Monkey swung his eyes to the fish-tanks.

"Don't you go near those goldfish!"

Monkey stood at bay, his eyes tacked hatefully on Berkeley, who ground his teeth, possessed by the sudden, wild desire to bite him, but knowing, finally, that he had the upper hand in the Pet Shoppe, the power. In other words, bigger teeth. As much as he hated to admit it, his only advantage, if he hoped to hold the line, his only trump, if he truly wanted to keep them afloat, was the fact that he outweighed them all. They were afraid of him. Oddly enough, the real validity of his values and viewpoint rested, he realized, on his having the biggest paw. The thought fretted him. For all his idealism, truth was decided in the end by those who could be bloodiest in fang and claw. Yet and still, Monkey had an arrogance that made Berkeley weak in the knees.

"Dog," he said, scratching under one arm, "you got to sleep *some*time."

And so Berkeley did. After hours of standing guard in the storeroom, or trying to console Rabbit, who was now talking of aborting the cabbit, begging her to reconsider, or reassuring the birds, who crowded together in one corner against, they said, threatening moves by the reptiles, or splashing various medicines on Frog, whose sickness had now spread to the iguana—after all this, Berkeley did drop fitfully to sleep by the front door. He slept greedily, dreaming of better days. He twitched and woofed in his sleep, seeing himself schtupping the little French poodle down the street, and it was

good, like making love to lightning, she moved so
well with him; and then of his puppyhood, when
his worst problems were remembering where he'd
buried food from Tilford's table, or figuring out
how to sneak away from his mother, who told him
all dogs had cold noses because they were late coming to the Ark and had to ride next to the rail. His
dream cycled on, as all dreams do, with greater and
greater clarity from one chamber of vision to the
next until he saw, just before waking, the final
drawer of dream-work spill open on the owner's
return. Splendidly dressed, wearing a bowler hat
and carrying a walking stick, sober, with a gentle
smile for Berkeley (Berkeley was sure), Tilford
threw open the Pet Shoppe door in a blast of wind
and burst of preternatural brilliance that rayed
the whole room, evaporated every shadow, and
brought the squabbling, the conflict of interpreta-
tions, mutations, and internecine battles to a halt.
No one dared move. They stood frozen like fish in
ice, or a bird caught in the crosswinds, the color-
less light behind the owner so blinding it obliterated
their outlines, blurred their precious differences,
as if each were a rill of the same ancient light
somehow imprisoned in form, with being-formed itself the most preposterous of conditions, outrageous, when you thought it through, because it occa-
sioned suffering, meant separation from other
forms, and the illusion of identity, but even this
ended like a dream within the watchdog's dream,

and only he and the owner remained. Reaching down, he stroked Berkeley's head. And at last he said, like God whispering to Samuel: *Well done.* It was all Berkeley had ever wanted. He woofed again, snoring like a sow, and scratched in his sleep; he heard the owner whisper *begun,* which was a pretty strange thing for him to say, even for Tilford, even in a dream. His ears strained forward; *begun,* Tilford said again. And for an instant Berkeley thought he had the tense wrong, intending to say, "Now we can begin," or something prophetically appropriate like that, but suddenly he was awake, and Parrot was flapping his wings and shouting into Berkeley's ear.

"The gun," said Parrot. "Monkey has it."

Berkeley's eyes, still phlegmed by sleep, blearily panned the counter. The room was swimming, full of smoke from a fire in the storeroom. He was short of wind. And, worse, he'd forgotten about the gun, a Smith and Wesson, that Tilford had bought after pet shop owners in Seattle were struck by thieves who specialized in stealing exotic birds. Monkey had it now. Berkeley's water ran down his legs. He'd propped the pistol between the cash register and a display of plastic dog collars, and his wide, yellow grin was frighteningly like that of a general Congress has just given the go-ahead to on a scorched-earth policy.

"Get it!" said Parrot. "You promised to protect us, Berkeley!"

For a few fibrous seconds he stood trembling paw-deep in dung, the odor of decay burning his lungs, but he couldn't come full awake, and still he felt himself to be on the fringe of a dream, his hair moist because dreaming of the French poodle had made him sweat. But the pistol . . . There was no power balance now. He'd been outplayed. No hope unless he took it away. Circling the counter, head low and growling, or trying to work up a decent growl, Berkeley crept to the cash register, his chest pounding, bunched his legs to leap, then sprang, pretending the black explosion of flame and smoke was like television gunfire, though it ripped skin right off his ribs, sent teeth flying down his throat, and blew him back like an empty pelt against Tortoise's cage. He lay still. Now he felt nothing in his legs. Purple blood like that deepest in the body cascaded to the floor from his side, rushing out with each heartbeat, and he lay twitching a little, only seeing now that he'd slept too long. Flames licked along the floor. Fish floated belly up in a dark, unplugged fishtank. The females had torn Siamese to pieces. Spackled lizards were busy sucking baby canaries from their eggs. And in the holy ruin of the Pet Shoppe the tarantula roamed free over the corpses of Frog and Iguana. Beneath him, Berkeley heard the ancient Tortoise stir, clearing a rusty throat clogged from disuse. Only he would survive the spreading fire, given his armor. His eyes burning from the smoke, the watchdog tried to explain his dream before the blaze reached them. "We could have endured, we had enough in common—for Christ's sake, we're *all* animals."

"Indeed," said Tortoise grimly, his eyes like headlights in a shell that echoed cavernously. "Indeed."

CHINA

If one man conquer in battle a thousand men, and if another conquers himself, he is the greatest of conquerors.

—*The Dhammapada*

Evelyn's problems with her husband, Rudolph, began one evening in early March—a dreary winter evening in Seattle—when he complained after a heavy meal of pig's feet and mashed potatoes of shortness of breath, an allergy to something she put in his food perhaps, or brought on by the first signs of wild flowers around them. She suggested they get out of the house for the evening, go to a movie. He was fifty-four, a postman for thirty-three years now, with high blood pressure, emphysema, flat feet, and, as Evelyn told her friend Shelberdine Lewis, the lingering fear that he had cancer. Getting old, he was also getting hard to live with. He told her never to salt his dinners, to keep their Lincoln Continental at a crawl, and never run her fingers along his inner thigh when they sat in Reverend William Merrill's church, because anything, even sex, or laughing too loud—Rudolph was serious—might bring on heart failure.

So she chose for their Saturday night outing a peaceful movie, a mildly funny comedy a *Seattle Times* reviewer said was fit only for titters and nasal snorts, a low-key satire that made Rudolph's eyelids droop as he shoveled down unbuttered popcorn in the darkened, half-empty theater. Sticky fluids cemented Evelyn's feet to the floor. A man in the last row laughed at all the wrong places. She kept the popcorn on her lap, though she hated the unsalted stuff and wouldn't touch it, sighing as Rudolph pawed across her to shove his fingers inside the cup.

She followed the film as best she could, but occasionally her eyes frosted over, flashed white. She went blind like this now and then. The fibers of her eyes were failing; her retinas were tearing like soft tissue. At these times the world was a canvas with whiteout spilling from the far left corner toward the center; it was the sudden shock of an empty frame in a series of slides. Someday, she knew, the snow on her eyes would stay. Winter eternally: her eyes split like her walking stick. She groped along the fractured surface, waiting for her sight to thaw, listening to the film she couldn't see. Her only comfort was knowing that, despite her infirmity, her Rudolph was in even worse health.

He slid back and forth from sleep during the film (she elbowed him occasionally, or pinched his leg), then came full awake, sitting up suddenly when the movie ended and a "Coming Attractions" trailer began. It was some sort of gladiator movie, Evelyn thought, blinking, and it was pretty trashy stuff at that. The plot's revenge theme was a poor excuse for Chinese actors or Japanese (she couldn't tell those people apart) to flail the air with their hands and feet, take on fifty costumed extras at once, and leap twenty feet through the air in perfect defiance of gravity. Rudolph's mouth hung open.

"Can people really do that?" He did not take his eyes off the screen, but talked at her from the right side of his mouth. "Leap that high?"

"It's a *movie*," sighed Evelyn. "A *bad* movie."

He nodded, then asked again, "But can they?"

"Oh, Rudolph, for God's sake!" She stood up to leave, her seat slapping back loudly. "They're on *trampolines*! You can see them in the corner— there!—if you open your eyes!"

He did see them, once Evelyn twisted his head to the lower left corner of the screen, and it seemed to her that her husband looked disappointed— looked, in fact, the way he did the afternoon Dr. Guylee told Rudolph he'd developed an extrasystolic reaction, a faint, moaning sound from his heart whenever it relaxed. He said no more and, after the trailer finished, stood—there was chew-

ing gum stuck to his trouser seat—dragged on his
heavy coat with her help and followed Evelyn up
the long, carpeted aisle, through the exit of the
Coronet Theater, and to their car. He said nothing
as she chattered on the way home, reminding him
that he could not stay up all night puttering in his
basement shop because the next evening they were
to attend the church's revival meeting.

Rudolph, however, did not attend the revival.
He complained after lunch of a light, dancing
pain in his chest, which he had conveniently whenever Mount Zion Baptist Church held revivals, and
she went alone, sitting with her friend Shelberdine,
a beautician. She was forty-one; Evelyn, fifty-two.
That evening Evelyn wore spotless white gloves,
tan therapeutic stockings for the swelling in her
ankles, and a white dress that brought out nicely
the brown color of her skin, the most beautiful
cedar brown, Rudolph said when they were court-
ing thirty-five years ago in South Carolina. But
then Evelyn had worn a matching checkered skirt
and coat to meeting. With her jet black hair pinned
behind her neck by a simple wooden comb, she
looked as if she might have been Andrew Wyeth's
starkly beautiful model for *Day of the Fair*. Rudolph, she remembered, wore black business suits,
black ties, black wing tips, but he also wore white
gloves because he was a senior usher—this was how
she first noticed him. He was one of four young
men dressed like deacons (or blackbirds), their

left hands tucked into the hollow of their backs, their right carrying silver plates for the offering as they marched in almost military fashion down each aisle: Christian soldiers, she'd thought, the cream of black manhood, and to get his attention she placed not her white envelope or coins in Rudolph's plate but instead a note that said: "You have a beautiful smile." It was, for all her innocence, a daring thing to do, according to Evelyn's mother—flirting with a randy young man like Rudolph Lee Jackson, but he did have nice, tigerish teeth. A killer smile, people called it, like all the boys in the Jackson family: a killer smile and good hair that needed no more than one stroke of his palm to bring out Quo Vadis rows pomaded sweetly with the scent of Murray's.

And, of course, Rudolph was no dummy. Not a total dummy, at least. He pretended nothing extraordinary had happened as the congregation left the little whitewashed church. He stood, the youngest son, between his father and mother, and let old Deacon Adcock remark, "Oh, how strong he's looking now," which was a lie. Rudolph was the weakest of the Jackson boys, the pale, bookish, spiritual child born when his parents were well past forty. His brothers played football, they went into the navy; Rudolph lived in Scripture, was labeled 4-F, and hoped to attend Moody Bible Institute in Chicago, if he could ever find the money. Evelyn could tell Rudolph knew exactly where she was in the crowd, that he could feel her as she and her sister, Debbie, waited for their father to bring his DeSoto—the family prize—closer to the front steps. When the crowd thinned, he shambled over in his slow, ministerial walk, introduced himself, and unfolded her note.

"You write this?" he asked. "It's not right to play with the Lord's money, you know."

"I like to play," she said.

"You do, huh?" He never looked directly at people. Women, she guessed, terrified him. Or, to be exact, the powerful emotions they caused in him terrified Rudolph. He was a pud puller, if she ever saw one. He kept his eyes on a spot left of her face. "You're Joe Montgomery's daughter, aren't you?"

"Maybe," teased Evelyn.

He trousered the note and stood marking the ground with his toe. "And just what you expect to get, Miss Playful, by fooling with people during collection time?"

She waited, let him look away, and, when the back-and-forth swing of his gaze crossed her again, said in her most melic, soft-breathing voice: "*You.*"

Up front, portly Reverend Merrill concluded his sermon. Evelyn tipped her head slightly, smiling into memory; her hand reached left to pat Rudolph's leg gently; then she remembered it was Shelberdine beside her, and lifted her hand to the seat in front of her. She said a prayer for Rudolph's health, but mainly it was for herself, a

hedge against her fear that their childless years
had slipped by like wind, that she might return
home one day and find him—as she had found her
father—on the floor, bellied up, one arm twisted
behind him where he fell, alone, his fingers locked
against his chest. Rudolph had begun to run down,
Evelyn decided, the minute he was turned down by
Moody Bible Institute. They moved to Seattle in
1956—his brother Eli was stationed nearby and
said Boeing was hiring black men. But they didn't
hire Rudolph. He had kidney trouble on and off
before he landed the job at the Post Office. Whenever he bent forward, he felt dizzy. Liver, heart,
and lungs—they'd worn down gradually as his
belly grew, but none of this was as bad as what he
called "the Problem." His pecker shrank to no bigger than a pencil eraser each time he saw her un-
dress. Or when Evelyn, as was her habit when
talking, touched his arm. Was she the cause of this?
Well, she knew she wasn't much to look at anymore.
She'd seen the bottom of a few too many candy
wrappers. Evelyn was nothing to make a man pant
and jump her bones, pulling her fully clothed onto
the davenport, as Rudolph had done years before,
but wasn't sex something else you surrendered with
age? It never seemed all that good to her anyway.
And besides, he'd wanted oral sex, which Evelyn—
if she knew nothing else—thought was a nasty,
unsanitary thing to do with your mouth. She
glanced up from under her spring hat past the

pulpit, past the choir of black and brown faces to the agonized beauty of a bearded white carpenter impaled on a rood, and in this timeless image she felt comforted that suffering was inescapable, the loss of vitality inevitable, even a good thing maybe, and that she had to steel herself—yes—for someday opening her bedroom door and finding her Rudolph face down in his breakfast oatmeal. He would die before her, she knew that in her bones.

And so, after service, Sanka, and a slice of meat pie with Shelberdine downstairs in the brightly lit church basement, Evelyn returned home to tell her husband how lovely the Griffin girls had sung that day, that their neighbor Rod Kenner had been saved, and to listen, if necessary, to Rudolph's fear that the lump on his shoulder was an early-warning sign of something evil. As it turned out, Evelyn found that except for their cat, Mr. Miller, the little A-frame house was empty. She looked in his bedroom. No Rudolph. The unnaturally still house made Evelyn uneasy, and she took the excruciatingly painful twenty stairs into the basement to peer into a workroom littered with power tools, planks of wood, and the blueprints her husband used to make bookshelves and cabinets. No Rudolph. Frightened, Evelyn called the eight hospitals in Seattle, but no one had a Rudolph Lee Jackson on his books. After her last call the starburst clock in the living room read twelve-thirty.

Putting down the wall phone, she felt a familiar pain in her abdomen. Another attack of Hershey squirts, probably from the meat pie. She hurried into the bathroom, lifted her skirt, and lowered her underwear around her ankles, but kept the door wide open, something impossible to do if Rudolph was home. Actually, it felt good not to have him underfoot, a little like he was dead already. But the last thing Evelyn wanted was that or, as she lay down against her lumpy backrest, to fall asleep, though she did, nodding off and dreaming until something shifted down her weight on the side of her bed away from the wall.

"Evelyn," said Rudolph, "look at this." She blinked back sleep and squinted at the cover of a magazine called *Inside Kung-Fu*, which Rudolph waved under her nose. On the cover a man stood bowlegged, one hand cocked under his armpit, the other corkscrewing straight at Evelyn's nose.

"Rudolph!" She batted the magazine aside, then swung her eyes toward the cluttered nightstand, focusing on the electric clock beside her water glass from McDonald's, Preparation H suppositories, and Harlequin romances. "It's morning!" Now she was mad. At least, working at it. "Where have you been?"

Her husband inhaled, a wheezing, whistlelike breath. He rolled the magazine into a cylinder and, as he spoke, struck his left palm with it. "That movie we saw advertised? You remember—it was called *The Five Fingers of Death*. I just saw that and one called *Deep Thrust*."

"Wonderful." Evelyn screwed up her lips. "I'm calling hospitals and you're at a Hong Kong double feature."

"Listen," said Rudolph. "You don't understand." He seemed at that moment as if he did not understand either. "It was a Seattle movie premiere. The Northwest is crawling with fighters. It has something to do with all the Asians out here. Before they showed the movie, four students from a kwoon in Chinatown went onstage—"

"A what?" asked Evelyn.

"A kwoon—it's a place to study fighting, a meditation hall." He looked at her but was really watching, Evelyn realized, something exciting she had missed. "They did a demonstration to drum up their membership. They broke boards and bricks, Evelyn. They went through what's called kata and kumite and . . ." He stopped again to breathe. "I've never seen anything so beautiful. The reason I'm late is because I wanted to talk with them after the movie."

Evelyn, suspicious, took a Valium and waited.

"I signed up for lessons," he said.

She gave a glacial look at Rudolph, then at his magazine, and said in the voice she used five years ago when he wanted to take a vacation to

Upper Volta or, before that, invest in a British car she knew they couldn't afford:

"You're fifty-*four* years old, Rudolph."

"I know that."

"You're no Muhammad Ali."

"I know that," he said.

"You're no Bruce Lee. Do you want to be Bruce Lee? Do you know where he is now, Rudolph? He'd dead—dead here in a Seattle cemetery and buried up on Capital Hill."

His shoulders slumped a little. Silently, Rudolph began undressing, his beefy backside turned toward her, slipping his pajama bottoms on before taking off his shirt so his scrawny lower body would not be fully exposed. He picked up his magazine, said, "I'm sorry if I worried you," and huffed upstairs to his bedroom. Evelyn clicked off the mushroom-shaped lamp on her nightstand. She lay on her side, listening to his slow footsteps strike the stairs, then heard his mattress creak above her— his bedroom was directly above hers—but she did not hear him click off his own light. From time to time she heard his shifting weight squeak the mattress springs. He was reading that foolish magazine, she guessed; then she grew tired and gave this impossible man up to God. With a copy of *The Thorn Birds* open on her lap, Evelyn fell heavily to sleep again.

At breakfast the next morning any mention of

the lessons gave Rudolph lockjaw. He kissed her forehead, as always, before going to work, and simply said he might be home late. Climbing the stairs to his bedroom was painful for Evelyn, but she hauled herself up, pausing at each step to huff, then sat on his bed and looked over his copy of *Inside Kung-Fu*. There were articles on empty-hand combat, soft-focus photos of ferocious-looking men in funny suits, parables about legendary Zen masters, an interview with someone named Bernie Bernheim, who began to study karate at age fifty-seven and became a black belt at age sixty-one, and page after page of advertisements for exotic Asian weapons: nunchaku, shuriken, sai swords, tonfa, bo staffs, training bags of all sorts, a wooden dummy shaped like a man and called a Mook Jong, and weights. Rudolph had circled them all. He had torn the order form from the last page of the magazine. The total cost of the things he'd circled—Evelyn added them furiously, rounding off the figures—was $800.

Two minutes later she was on the telephone to Shelberdine.

"Let him tire of it," said her friend. "Didn't you tell me Rudolph had Lower Lombard Strain?"

Evelyn's nose clogged with tears.

"Why is he doing this? Is it me, do you think?"

"It's the Problem," said Shelberdine. "He wants his manhood back. Before he died, Arthur did the same. Someone at the plant told him he

74

could get it back if he did twenty-yard sprints. He went into convulsions while running around the lake."

Evelyn felt something turn in her chest. "You don't think he'll hurt himself, do you?"

"Of course not."

"Do you think he'll hurt *me*?"

Her friend reassured Evelyn that Mid-Life Crisis brought out these shenanigans in men. Evelyn replied that she thought Mid-Life Crisis started around age forty, to which Shelberdine said, "Honey, I don't mean no harm, but Rudolph always was a little on the slow side," and Evelyn agreed. She would wait until he worked this thing out of his system, until Nature defeated him and he surrendered, as any right-thinking person would, to the breakdown of the body, the brutal fact of decay, which could only be blunted, it seemed to her, by decaying *with* someone, the comfort every Negro couple felt when, aging, they knew enough to let things wind down.

Her patience was rewarded in the beginning. Rudolph crawled home from his first lesson, hunched over, hardly able to stand, afraid he had permanently ruptured something. He collapsed face down on the living room sofa, his feet on the floor. She helped him change into his pajamas and fingered Ben-Gay into his back muscles. Evelyn had never seen her husband so close to tears.

"I can't *do* push-ups," he moaned. "Or sit-ups. I'm so stiff—I don't know my body." He lifted his head, looking up pitifully, his eyes pleading. "Call Dr. Guylee. Make an appointment for Thursday, okay?"

"Yes, dear." Evelyn hid her smile with one hand. "You shouldn't push yourself so hard."

At that, he sat up, bare-chested, his stomach bubbling over his pajama bottoms. "That's what it means. *Gung-fu* means 'hard work' in Chinese. Evelyn"—he lowered his voice—"I don't think I've ever really done hard work in my life. Not like this, something that asks me to give *every*thing, body and soul, spirit and flesh. I've always felt . . ." He looked down, his dark hands dangling between his thighs. "I've never been able to give *every*thing to *any*thing. The world never let me. It won't let me put all of myself into play. Do you know what I'm saying? Every job I've ever had, everything I've ever done, it only demanded part of me. It was like there was so much *more* of me that went unused after the job was over. I get that feeling in church sometimes." He lay back down, talking now into the sofa cushion. "Sometimes I get that feeling with you."

Her hand stopped on his shoulder. She wasn't sure she'd heard him right, his voice was so muffled. "That I've never used all of you?"

Rudolph nodded, rubbing his right knuckle where, at the kwoon, he'd lost a stretch of skin on a speedbag. "There's still part of me left over.

You never tried to touch all of me, to take everything. Maybe you can't. Maybe no one can. But sometimes I get the feeling that the unused part—the unlived life—*spoils*, that you get cancer because it sits like fruit on the ground and rots." Rudolph shook his head; he'd said too much and knew it, perhaps had not even put it the way he felt inside. Stiffly, he got to his feet. "Don't ask me to stop training." His eyebrows spread inward. "If I stop, I'll die."

Evelyn twisted the cap back onto the Ben-Gay. She held out her hand, which Rudolph took. Veins on the back of his hand burgeoned abnormally like dough. Once when she was shopping at the Public Market she'd seen monstrous plastic gloves shaped like hands in a magic store window. His hand looked like that. It belonged on Lon Chaney. Her voice shook a little, panicky, "I'll call Dr. Guylee in the morning."

Evelyn knew—or thought she knew—his trouble. He'd never come to terms with the disagreeableness of things. Rudolph had always been too serious for some people, even in South Carolina. It was the thing, strange to say, that drew her to him, this crimped-browed tendency in Rudolph to listen with every atom of his life when their minister in Hodges, quoting Marcus Aurelius to give his sermon flash, said, "Live with the gods," or later in Seattle, the habit of working himself up over Reverend Merrill's reading from Ecclesiastes 9:10: "Whatsoever thy hand findeth to do, do it with all thy might." Now, he didn't *really* mean that, Evelyn knew. Nothing in the world could be taken that seriously; that's *why* this was the world. And, as all Mount Zion knew, Reverend Merrill had a weakness for high-yellow choirgirls and gin, and was forever complaining that his salary was too small for his family. People made compromises, nodded at spiritual commonplaces—the high seriousness of biblical verses that demanded nearly superhuman duty and selfdenial—and laughed off their lapses into sloth, envy, and the other deadly sins. It was what made living so enjoyably *human*: this built-in inability of man to square his performance with perfection. People were naturally soft on themselves. But not her Rudolph.

Of course, he seldom complained. It was not in his nature to complain when, looking for "gods," he found only ruin and wreckage. What did he expect? Evelyn wondered. Man was evil—she'd told him that a thousand times—or, if not evil, hopelessly flawed. Everything failed; it was some sort of law. But at least there was laughter, and lovers clinging to one another against the cliff; there were novels—wonderful tales of how things should be—and perfection promised in the afterworld. He'd sit and listen, her Rudolph, when she put things this way, nodding because he knew that in his persistent hunger for perfection in the here and now he was,

at best, in the minority. He kept his dissatisfaction
to himself, but occasionally Evelyn would glimpse
in his eyes that look, that distant, pained expression that asked: *Is this all?* She saw it after her
first miscarriage, then her second; saw it when he
stopped searching the want ads and settled on the
Post Office as the fulfillment of his potential in the
marketplace. It was always there, that look, after
he turned forty, and no new, lavishly praised novel
from the Book-of-the-Month Club, no feature-
length movie, prayer meeting, or meal she fixed
for him wiped it from Rudolph's eyes. He was, at
least, this sort of man before he saw that martial-
arts B movie. It was a dark vision, Evelyn decided,
a dangerous vision, and in it she whiffed something
that might destroy her. What that was, she couldn't
say, but she knew her Rudolph better than he knew
himself. He would see the error—the waste of
time—in his new hobby, and she was sure he would
mend his ways.

In the weeks, then months that followed Evelyn waited, watching her husband for a flag of surrender. There was no such sign. He became worse
than before. He cooked his own meals, called her
heavy soul food dishes "too acidic," lived on raw
vegetables, seaweed, nuts, and fruit to make his
body "more alkaline," and fasted on Sundays. He
ordered books on something called Shaolin fighting
and meditation from a store in California, and
when his equipment arrived UPS from Dolan's

Sports in New Jersey, he ordered more—in con-
sternation, Evelyn read the list—leg stretchers,
makiwara boards, air shields, hand grips, bokken,
focus mitts, a full-length mirror (for heaven's
sake) so he could correct his form, and protective
equipment. For proper use of his headgear and
gloves, however, he said he needed a sparring part-
ner—an opponent—he said, to help him instinctively understand "combat strategy," how to "flow"
and "close the Gap" between himself and an ad-
versary, how to create by his movements a negative
space in which the other would be neutralized.

"Well," crabbed Evelyn, "if you need a
punching bag, don't look at *me*."

He sat across the kitchen table from her, doing
dynamic-tension exercises as she read a new magazine called *Self*. "Did I ever tell you what a black
belt means?" he asked.

"You told me."

"Sifu Chan doesn't use belts for ranking. They
were introduced seventy years ago because West-
erners were impatient, you know, needed signposts
and all that."

"You told me," said Evelyn.

"Originally, all you got was a white belt. It
symbolized innocence. Virginity." His face was im-
mensely serious, like a preacher's. "As you worked,
it got darker, dirtier, and turned brown. Then
black. You were a master then. With even more

work, the belt became frayed, the threads came loose, you see, and the belt showed white again."

"Rudolph, I've heard this before!" Evelyn picked up her magazine and took it into her bedroom. From there, with her legs drawn up under the blankets, she shouted: "I *won't* be your punching bag!"

So he brought friends from his kwoon, friends she wanted nothing to do with. There was something unsettling about them. Some were street fighters. Young. They wore tank-top shirts and motorcycle jackets. After drinking racks of Rainier beer on the front porch, they tossed their crumpled empties next door into Rod Kenner's yard. Together, two of Rudolph's new friends—Truck and Tuco—weighed a quarter of a ton. Evelyn kept a rolling pin under her pillow when they came, but she knew they could eat that along with her. But some of his new friends were students at the University of Washington. Truck, a Vietnamese only two years in America, planned to apply to the Police Academy once his training ended; and Tuco, who was Puerto Rican, had been fighting since he could make a fist; but a delicate young man named Andrea, a blue sash, was an actor in the drama department at the university. His kwoon training, he said, was less for self-defense than helping him understand his movements onstage—how, for example, to convincingly explode across a room in anger. Her husband liked them, Evelyn realized in horror. And they liked him. They were separated by money, background, and religion, but something she could not identify made them seem, those nights on the porch after his class, like a single body. They called Rudolph "Older Brother" or, less politely, "Pop."

His sifu, a short, smooth-figured boy named Douglas Chan, who Evelyn figured couldn't be over eighteen, sat like the Dalai Lama in their tiny kitchen as if he owned it, sipping her tea, which Rudolph laced with Korean ginseng. Her husband lit Chan's cigarettes as if he were President Carter come to visit the common man. He recommended that Rudolph study T'ai Chi, "soft" fighting systems, ki, and something called Tao. He told him to study, as well, Newton's three laws of physics and apply them to his own body during kumite. What she remembered most about Chan were his wrist braces, ornamental weapons that had three straps and, along the black leather, highly polished studs like those worn by Steve Reeves in a movie she'd seen about Hercules. In a voice she thought girlish, he spoke of eye gouges and groin-tearing techniques, exercises called the Delayed Touch of Death and Dim Mak, with the casualness she and Shelberdine talked about bargains at Thriftway. And then they suited up, the boyish Sifu, who looked like Maharaj-ji's rougher brother, and her clumsy husband; they went out back, pushed aside the aluminum lawn furniture, and pommeled each other for half an hour. More precisely, her Rudolph was on the receiving end of hook kicks, spinning back fists faster than thought, and foot sweeps that left his body purpled for weeks. A sensible man would have known enough to drive to Swedish Hospital pronto. Rudolph, never known as a profound thinker, pushed on after Sifu Chan left, practicing his flying kicks by leaping to ground level from a four-foot hole he'd dug by their cyclone fence.

Evelyn, nibbling a Van de Kamp's pastry from Safeway—she was always nibbling, these days—watched from the kitchen window until twilight, then brought out the Ben-Gay, a cold beer, and rubbing alcohol on a tray. She figured he needed it. Instead, Rudolph, stretching under the far-reaching cedar in the backyard, politely refused, pushed the tray aside, and rubbed himself with Dit-Da-Jow, "iron-hitting wine," which smelled like the open door of an opium factory on a hot summer day. Yet this ancient potion not only instantly healed his wounds (said Rudolph) but prevented arthritis as well. She was tempted to see if it healed brain damage by pouring it into Rudolph's ears, but apparently he was doing something right. Dr. Guylee's examination had been glowing; he said Rudolph's muscle tone, whatever that was, was better. His cardiovascular system was healthier. His erections were outstanding—or upstanding—though lately he seemed to have no interest in sex. Evelyn, even she, saw in the crepuscular light changes in Rudolph's upper body as he stretched: Muscles like globes of light rippled along his shoulders; larval currents moved on his belly. The language of his new, developing body eluded her. He was not always like this. After a cold shower and sleep his muscles shrank back a little. It was only after his workouts, his weight lifting, that his body expanded like baking bread, filling out in a way that obliterated the soft Rudolph-body she knew. This new flesh had the contours of the silhouetted figures on medical charts: the body as it must be in the mind of God. Glistening with perspiration, his muscles took on the properties of the free weights he pumped relentlessly. They were profoundly tragic, too, because their beauty was earthbound. It would vanish with the world. You are ugly, his new muscles said to Evelyn; old and ugly. His self-punishment made her feel sick. She was afraid of his hard, cold weights. She hated them. Yet she wanted them, too. They had a certain monastic beauty. She thought: *He's doing this to hurt me.* She wondered: What was it like to be powerful? Was clever cynicism—even comedy—the by-product of bulging bellies, weak nerves, bad posture? Her only defense against the dumbbells that stood between them—she meant both his weights and his friends—was, as always, her acid southern tongue:

"They're all fairies, right?"

Rudolph looked dreamily her way. These post-workout periods made him feel, he said, as if there were no interval between himself and what he saw. His face was vacant, his eyes—like smoke. In this afterglow (he said) he saw without judging. Without judgment, there were no distinctions. Without distinctions, there was no desire. Without desire . . .

He smiled sideways at her. "Who?"

"The people in your kwoon." Evelyn crossed her arms. "I read somewhere that most body builders are homosexual."

He refused to answer her.

"If they're not gay, then maybe I should take lessons. It's been good for you, right?" Her voice grew sharp. "I mean, isn't that what you're saying? That you and your friends are better'n everybody else?"

Rudolph's head dropped; he drew a long breath. Lately, his responses to her took the form of quietly clearing his lungs.

"You should do what you *have* to, Evelyn. You don't have to do what anybody else does." He stood up, touched his toes, then brought his forehead straight down against his unbent knees, which was physically impossible, Evelyn would have said—and faintly obscene.

It was a nightmare to watch him each evening after dinner. He walked around the house in his Everlast leg weights, tried push-ups on his finger-

tips and wrists, and, as she sat trying to watch
"The Jeffersons," stood in a ready stance before
the flickering screen, throwing punches each time
the scene, or shot, changed to improve his timing.
It took the fun out of watching TV, him doing
that—she preferred him falling asleep in his chair
beside her, as he used to. But what truly frightened
Evelyn was his "doing nothing." Sitting in meditation, planted cross-legged in a full lotus on their
front porch, with Mr. Miller blissfully curled on
his lap, a Bodhisattva in the middle of houseplants
she set out for the sun. Looking at him, you'd have
thought he was dead. The whole thing smelled like
self-hypnosis. He breathed too slowly, in Evelyn's
view—only three breaths per minute, he claimed.
He wore his gi, splotchy with dried blood and sweat,
his calloused hands on his knees, the forefingers on
each tipped against his thumbs, his eyes screwed
shut.

During his eighth month at the kwoon, she
stood watching him as he sat, wondering over the
vivid changes in his body, the grim firmness where
before there was jolly fat, the disquieting steadi-
ness of his posture, where before Rudolph could not
sit still in church for five minutes without fidgeting.
Now he sat in zazen for forty-five minutes a day,
fifteen when he awoke, fifteen (he said) at work in
the mailroom during his lunch break, fifteen before going to bed. He called this withdrawal (how
she hated his fancy language) similar to the neces-

sary silences in music, "a stillness that prepared him for busyness and sound." He'd never breathed before, he told her. Not once. Not clear to the floor of himself. Never breathed and emptied himself as he did now, picturing himself sitting on the bottom of Lake Washington: himself, Rudolph Lee Jackson, at the center of the universe; for if the universe was infinite, any point where he stood would be at its center—it would shift and move with him. (That saying, Evelyn knew, was minted in Douglas Chan's mind. No Negro preacher worth the name would speak that way.) He told her that in zazen, at the bottom of the lake, he worked to discipline his mind and maintain one point of concentration; each thought, each feeling that overcame him he saw as a fragile bubble, which he could inspect passionlessly from all sides; then he let it float gently to the surface, and soon—as he slipped deeper into the vortices of himself, into the Void—even the image of himself on the lake floor vanished.

Evelyn stifled a scream.

Was she one of Rudolph's bubbles, something to detach himself from? On the porch, Evelyn watched him narrowly, sitting in a rain-whitened chair, her chin on her left fist. She snapped the fingers on her right hand under his nose. Nothing. She knocked her knuckles lightly on his forehead. Nothing. (Faker, she thought.) For another five minutes he sat and breathed, sat and breathed, then opened his eyes slowly as if he'd slept as long as Rip

Van Winkle. "It's dark," he said, stunned. When he began, it was twilight. Evelyn realized something new: He was not living time as she was, not even that anymore. Things, she saw, were slower for him; to him she must seem like a woman stuck in fast-forward. She asked:

"What do you see when you go in there?"

Rudolph rubbed his eyes. "Nothing."

"Then *why* do you do it? The world's out here!"

He seemed unable to say, as if the question were senseless. His eyes angled up, like a child's, toward her face. "Nothing is peaceful sometimes. The emptiness is full. I'm not afraid of it now."

"You empty yourself?" she asked. "Of me, too?"

"Yes."

Evelyn's hand shot up to cover her face. She let fly with a whimper. Rudolph rose instantly—he sent Mr. Miller flying—then fell back hard on his buttocks; the lotus cut off blood to his lower body—which provided more to his brain, he claimed—and it always took him a few seconds before he could stand again. He reached up, pulled her hand down, and stroked it.

"What've I done?"

"That's it," sobbed Evelyn. "I don't know what you're doing." She lifted the end of her bathrobe, blew her nose, then looked at him through streaming, unseeing eyes. "And you don't either.

I wish you'd never seen that movie. I'm sick of all
your weights and workouts—sick of them, do you
hear? Rudolph, I want you back the way you were:
sick." No sooner than she said this Evelyn was
sorry. But she'd done no harm. Rudolph, she saw,
didn't want anything; everything, Evelyn included,
delighted him, but as far as Rudolph was con-
cerned, it was all shadows in a phantom history.
He was humbler now, more patient, but he'd lost
touch with everything she knew was normal in people: weakness, fear, guilt, self-doubt, the very
things that gave the world thickness and made
people do things. She *did* want him to desire her.
No, she didn't. Not if it meant oral sex. Evelyn
didn't know, really, what she wanted anymore. She
felt, suddenly, as if she might dissolve before his
eyes. "Rudolph, if you're 'empty,' like you say, you
don't know who—or what—is talking to you. If
you said you were praying, I'd understand. It
would be God talking to you. But this way . . ."
She pounded her fist four, five times on her thigh.
"It could be *evil* spirits, you know! There *are* evil
spirits, Rudolph. It could be the Devil."

Rudolph thought for a second. His chest lowered after another long breath. "Evelyn, this is
going to sound funny, but I don't believe in the
Devil."

Evelyn swallowed. It had come to that.

"Or God—unless we are gods."

She could tell he was at pains to pick his

words carefully, afraid he might offend. Since joining the kwoon and studying ways to kill, he seemed particularly careful to avoid her own most effective weapon: the wry, cutting remark, the put-down, the direct, ego-deflating slash. Oh, he was becoming a real saint. At times, it made her want to hit him.

"Whatever is just *is*," he said. "That's all I know. Instead of worrying about whether it's good or bad, God or the Devil, I just want to be quiet, work on myself, and interfere with things as little as possible. Evelyn," he asked suddenly, "how can there be *two* things?" His brow wrinkled; he chewed his lip. "You think what I'm saying is evil, don't you?"

"I think it's strange! Rudolph, you didn't grow up in China," she said. "They can't breathe in China! I saw that today on the news. They burn soft coal, which gets into the air and turns into acid rain. They wear face masks over there, like the ones we bought when Mount St. Helens blew up. They all ride bicycles, for Christ's sake! They want what we have." Evelyn heard Rod Kenner step onto his screened porch, perhaps to listen from his rocker. She dropped her voice a little. "You grew up in Hodges, South Carolina, same as me, in a right and proper colored church. If you'd *been* to China, maybe I'd understand."

"I can only be what I've been?" This he asked

softly, but his voice trembled. "Only what I was in Hodges?"

"You can't be Chinese."

"I don't want to be Chinese!" The thought made Rudolph smile and shake his head. Because she did not understand, and because he was tired of talking, Rudolph stepped back a few feet from her, stretching again, always stretching. "I only want to be what I *can* be, which isn't the greatest fighter in the world, only the fighter *I* can be. Lord knows, I'll probably get creamed in the tournament this Saturday." He added, before she could reply, "Doug asked me if I'd like to compete this weekend in full-contact matches with some people from the kwoon. I have to." He opened the screen door. "I will."

"You'll be killed—you know that, Rudolph." She dug her fingernails into her bathrobe, and dug this into him: "You know, you never were very strong. Six months ago you couldn't open a pickle jar for me."

He did not seem to hear her. "I bought a ticket for you." He held the screen door open, waiting for her to come inside. "I'll fight better if you're there."

She spent the better part of that week at Shelberdine's mornings and Reverend Merrill's church evenings, rinsing her mouth with prayer, sitting most often alone in the front row so she

would not have to hear Rudolph talking to himself
from the musty basement as he pounded out bench
presses, skipped rope for thirty minutes in the
backyard, or shadowboxed in preparation for a
fight made inevitable by his new muscles. She had
married a fool, that was clear, and if he expected
her to sit on a bench at the Kingdome while some
equally stupid brute spilled the rest of his brains—
probably not enough left now to fill a teaspoon—
then he was wrong. How could he see the world as
"perfect"?—That was his claim. There was pov-
erty, unemployment, twenty-one children dying
every minute, every day, every year from hunger
and malnutrition, over twenty murdered in At-
lanta; there were sixty thousand nuclear weapons
in the world, which was dreadful, what with Seattle
so close to Boeing; there were far-right Republi-
cans in the White House: *good* reasons, Evelyn
thought, to be "negative and life-denying," as Rudolph would put it. It was almost sin to see harmony
in an earthly hell, and in a fit of spleen she prayed
God would dislocate his shoulder, do some minor
damage to humble him, bring him home, and re-
mind him that the body was vanity, a violation of
every verse in the Bible. But Evelyn could not sus-
tain her thoughts as long as he could. Not for more
than a few seconds. Her mind never settled, never
rested, and finally on Saturday morning, when she
awoke on Shelberdine's sofa, it would not stay away
from the image of her Rudolph dead before hun-

dreds of indifferent spectators, paramedics pounding on his chest, bursting his rib cage in an effort
to keep him alive.

From Shelberdine's house she called a taxi
and, in the steady rain that northwesterners love,
arrived at the Kingdome by noon. It's over already,
Evelyn thought, walking the circular stairs to her
seat, clamping shut her wet umbrella. She heard
cheers, booing, an Asian voice with an accent over
a microphone. The tournament began at ten, which
was enough time for her white belt husband to be
in the emergency ward at Harborview Hospital by
now, but she had to see. At first, as she stepped
down to her seat through the crowd, she could only
hear—her mind grappled for the word, then remembered—kiais, or "spirit shouts," from the great
floor of the stadium, many shouts, for contests were
progressing in three rings simultaneously. It felt
like a circus. It smelled like a locker room. Here
two children stood toe to toe until one landed a
front kick that sent the other child flying fifteen
feet. There two lean-muscled female black belts
were interlocked in a delicate ballet, like dance or
a chess game, of continual motion. They had a
kind of sense, these women—she noticed it immediately—a feel for space and their place in it.
(Evelyn hated them immediately.) And in the
farthest circle she saw, or rather felt, Rudolph, the
oldest thing on the deck, who, sparring in the adult
division, was squared off with another white belt,

not a boy who might hurt him—the other man was middle-aged, graying, maybe only a few years younger than Rudolph—but they were sparring just the same.

Yet it was not truly him that Evelyn, sitting down, saw. Acoustics in the Kingdome whirlpooled the noise of the crowd, a rivering of voices that affected her, suddenly, like the pitch and roll of voices during service. It affected the way she watched Rudolph. She wondered: Who are these people? She caught her breath when, miscalculating his distance from his opponent, her husband stepped sideways into a roundhouse kick with lots of snap—she heard the cloth of his opponent's gi crack like a gunshot when he threw the technique. She leaned forward, gripping the huge purse on her lap when Rudolph recovered and retreated from the killing to the neutral zone, and then, in a wide stance, rethought strategy. This was not the man she'd slept with for twenty years. Not her hypochondriac Rudolph who had to rest and run cold water on his wrists after walking from the front stairs to the fence to pick up the *Seattle Times*. She did not know him, perhaps had never known him, and now she never would, for the man on the floor, the man splashed with sweat, rising on the ball of his rear foot for a flying kick—was he so foolish he still thought he could fly?—would outlive her; he'd stand healthy and strong and think of her in a bubble, one hand on her headstone, and it was all

right, she thought, weeping uncontrollably, it was
all right that Rudolph would return home after
visiting her wet grave, clean out her bedroom, the
pillboxes and paperback books, and throw open her
windows to let her sour, rotting smell escape, then
move a younger woman's things onto the floor
space darkened by her color television, her porce-
lain chamber pot, her antique sewing machine. And
then Evelyn was on her feet, unsure why, but the
crowd had stood suddenly to clap, and Evelyn
clapped, too, though for an instant she pounded
her gloved hands together instinctively until her
vision cleared, the momentary flash of retinal blind-
ness giving way to a frame of her husband, the
postman, twenty feet off the ground in a perfect
flying kick that floored his opponent and made a
Japanese judge who looked like Oddjob shout
"ippon"—one point—and the fighting in the farthest ring, in herself, perhaps in all the world,
was over.

ALĒTHIA

God willing, I'm going to tell you a love story. A skeptical old man, whose great forehead and gray forked beard most favor (when I flatter myself) those of that towering sociologist W. E. B. Du Bois, I am hardly a man to conjure a fabulation so odd in its transfiguration of things, so strange, so terrifying (thus it now seems to me) that it belongs on the pale lips of the poetic genius who wrote *Essentials* and that hallucinatory prose-poem called *Cane*. But even though I'm an old man (I know my faults: failing memory, an infernal Faustian leer), I can still tell a first-rate tale of romance.

The girl always came late to my evening seminar—Kant this semester—sashaying seduc-

tively, pulled into the room by rental-library books
held close to her chest, clomping in black leather
boots around the long table to sit, her brown knees
pressed together, left of my lectern. When she first
"appeared" to me, I believe I was stalking Kant,
thumbs hooked in my vest, by way of a playful
verse attributed to Bishop Berkeley:

> There was a young man who felt God
> Must find it exceedingly odd
> > When he finds that this tree
> > Continues to be
> When there's no one about in the Quad.

> "Dear sir, your astonishment's odd;
> I am always about in the Quad.
> > And, therefore, this tree
> > Will continue to be
> As observed by yours, faithfully, God."

Lecturing, I seldom noticed her, only a dark
blur, a whiff of sandalwood, but this winter, after
thirty years of teaching, years as outwardly calm
as those of a monk or contemplative, devoted to
books, my study of Kant led to a nearly forgotten
philosopher named Max Scheler, who said—and
this shook me deeply—"Contemplation of essence,
the fundamental approach to Being peculiar to
metaphysical knowledge, demands an attitude of
loving devotion," so yes, I did see Wendy Barnes,

but with the flash of clear vision, the focus, the gasp of recognition that slaps you, suddenly, when a tree drawing in a child's book (the dome of leaves, I mean) recomposes itself as a face. My mouth wobbled. If I had been standing, I would have staggered. I forgot my lecture; I sent my Kant scholars home.

Legging it back to my office in Padelford Hall, a building as old—so I put it to myself—as a medieval fortress, I could not pull my thoughts together. *Shame*, I thought. *O shameful* to have hot flashes for a student. My room of papers (half-finished books that had collapsed on me in mid-manuscript, or changed as I was chasing them), closed 'round me comfortably when I slumped behind my desk, flipping through my gradebook. The girl Wendy, an Equal Opportunity Program student, was failing—no fault of mine—but it saddened me all the same, and now I suppose I must tell you why.

Time being short, I must explain briefly, hoping not to bore you, that a Negro professor is, although reappointed and tenured, a kind of two-reel comedy. Like his students, like Wendy, he looks back to the bleak world of black Chicago (in my case), where his spirit, if you will, fought to free itself—as Hegel's anxious Spirit struggles against matter—from a life that led predictably to either (a) drugs, (b) a Post Office job, (c) Marion Prison, (d) Sunset Cemetery (all black),

or (e) the ooga-booga of Christianity. And what
of college? There, like a thief come to table, he
hungrily grabs crumbs of thought from their
genuine context, reading Hume for his reasoning
on the self, blinking that author's racial slurs,
"feeling his twoness," as Du Bois so beautifully put
it in a brilliant stroke of classic Dualism, "an
American, a Negro; two souls, two thoughts, two
warring ideals in one dark body." Regardless, he
puts his shoulder to the wheel, pushing doggedly
on as I did: a dreamy, first-generation student in
a paint-by-numbers curriculum, fed by books for
Negro uplift—the modern equivalent, you might
say, of Plutarch's *Lives of the Noble Grecians*
(which I swore by). Not exactly biography, these
odd books from the Negro press, and with titles
like *Lives That Lift*—written by blacks to inspire
blacks—but myths about men who tried, in their
own small way, to create lives that could be, if dis-
ciplined, the basis of universal law. He embraces—
and this is the killing part—the lofty balderdash
of his balding, crabbed-faced teachers about sober
Truth and Science when they, shaken by Wittgen-
stein, had in fact lost faith and were madly hump-
ing their teaching assistants.

So, I mean to say, that Scheler, the night before in my study, pulled me up short. Lately, I live
alone in three untidy, low-ceilinged rooms I rent
in Evanston near Northwestern University. I get
up at three each morning, read Hebrew, Greek, or

Sanskrit at my roll-top desk, but no tabloids or
lurid newspapers. Nights, I soak in a hot bath of
Epsom salts, never forget my thought exercises—
perceptual tricks pulled from Husserl's *Ideen*—
and eat my dinners (no meat or eggs) in a nearby
diner, slowly because I have an ulcer, bad diges-
tion, and a bathroom cabinet spilling open with
pills for migraines, stomach cramps, and potions
(Dr. Hobson's Vegetable Prescription, McClean's
Tar Wine Compound) for rest. At fifty, I sleep
poorly. So it has been for years. Barricaded in by
books, bleary with insomnia, I read Scheler's *Philosophical Perspectives*, my medicines beside me on
my desk, and it came to me, sadly—I felt sad,
at least, as if I'd misunderstood something any
salesgirl knew instinctively—that living for knowledge, ignoring love, as I had, was wrong, because
love—transcendental love—*was* knowledge. True
enough, "love" is on the lips of every sentimental
schoolgirl (or boy), and cheapened by maudlin
songwriters. A thoughtful man doubts, and rightly
so, these vulgar reports.

But Scheler wrote—if I've got this right—
that Mind, revealed by Kant to be only a relation
in the worldweb, was a special kind of window, a
gap in Being, an opening that, if directed toward
another, allowed him (or her) to appear—like
Plato's form of "The Good"—as both moral and
beautiful. The implications, I daresay, were stag-
gering, for Nature, contrary to common sense,

needed man to clarify its meaning. (Of course, there was a paradox in this: To say "Man clarifies Nature" is to say, oddly, that "Nature clarifies Nature," because man is a part of Nature, which suggests, stranger still, that man—if self-forgetful—is not an actor or agent at all.) Scheler's happy term *alēthia*, "to call forth from concealedness," advanced the theory that each man, each moment, each blink of the eye, was responsible for obliterating the petty "Old Adam" and conjuring only those visions from perceptual chaos that *let be* goodness, truth, beauty. So what? So this:

How a better scholar would interpret this, I do not know; but to a plodding, tired man like myself, *alēthia* meant the celebration of exactly that ugly, lovely black life (so it was to me) I'd fled so long ago in my childhood, as if seeing beauty in every tissue and every vein of a world lacking discipline and obedience to law were the real goal of metaphysics; as if, for all my hankering after Truth in the Academy, Truth had been hidden all along, waiting for my "look" in the cold-water flats between Cottage Grove Avenue and the Rock Island right-of-way.

I was under the spell of this extravagant idea when Wendy Barnes came barreling into my office, sore as hell, banging the door against my wall, and blew noisily up to my desk. "You know what my adviser, the punk, just pulled on me?" She was chewing gum with her mouth open, punishing the wad as if it might be her adviser.

"There now," I said, professorial. I pushed back my swivel chair. "Tell me about it."

She slammed shut the door with her hip, then threw herself into a chair. Here then was Wendy in a loose white blouse and open-top brassiere, with a floss of black hair, a wide, thick mouth, and a loud, vibrating voice. I judged her to be twenty-five. She had large, uncanny eyes that sometimes looked brown or sepia, sometimes black with no iris like blobs of oil, sometimes hard and gray like metal. And what of her character? She might have been one of three sassy, well-medicated blues singers backing up James Brown down at the Regal. I thought her vulgar. "I've got to get a B to stay in school." She dipped into her purse for a pack of Kools—"Or they kick me out, see?—then lit a cigarette. Her hands shook, bobbling the flame of her match; then she lifted her head, slanting her eyes at me. "I'll do *any*thing to get that grade."

"Anything?" I asked. "Perhaps an incomplete for—"

"You still don't get it, do you?" She blinked away cigarette smoke curling up her wrist. "Like, I been here goin' on six years now, and if nothing else, I know how this place works. Like, I ain't got nothin' against you, but I ain't *about* to go back to no factory, or day-work. If I don't ace this

course—are you listenin'?—I'm gonna have to tell
your chairman Dick Dunn and Dean David Mc-
Cracken that you been houndin' me for trim."

"Me?" I looked up. "Trim?"

"Look"—from my desk she lifted a fountain
pen—"I'll give you an ostensive definition." Un-
capping it, she slowly slid the pen back into the
cap. "See?"

Lord, I thought. *O Lord.*

"Like, it's nothin' personal, though." She was
at pains to keep this catastrophe on a friendly
basis. Aboveboard. "But if *I* flunk," she said,
"you're finished." Then, like a trap door, Wendy's
face sprang open in a beautiful smile. She touched
my hand. "I *can* be nice, too, you know, once you
get to know me."

I didn't believe her. She'd have to be crazy to
say this. It was, for a timid Negro professor who
never thought of using his position for leverage,
an all-hands-to-the-pump panic. My heart started
banging away; I could not snap the room into
clarity. She was armed with endless tricks and
strategies, this black girl, but Wendy was nobody's
fool—she used Niggerese playfully, like a toy,
to bait, to draw me out. She was a witch, yes. A
thug. But she had me, rightly or wrongly, at bay.
I drew deeply for air. I asked, fighting to steady
my voice, "You'd do this?"

"Yeah," she said. Her nose twitched. "Mrs.

Barnes's baby daughter is strictly business tonight." And then: "Say what you're thinkin'."

My voice shattered. "I haven't *done* anything!
Nothing! Not to you. Or anyone! Or—"

"So don't be stupid." She was standing now,
crushing out her cigarette. Her blouse pulled
tightly against her bosom. "My mama only got as
far as second grade, but she always said, 'If you
gonna be accused of somethin', you might as well
do it.' " She smiled. Deep in my stomach I felt sick.
What I felt, in fact, was trapped. Rage as I might,
I felt, strangely, that this disaster was somehow
all my own doing. Now she opened the office door.
"Can we go someplace and talk? Do you hang out?"

Although I do not "hang out" (I checked my
fly to make sure), she pulled me in tow downstairs
to her sports car, clicked on her tape deck, then
accelerated along the Lake Michigan shoreline, her
speedometer right on seventy, damned near blow-
ing off both doors, then tooled down Wacker Drive.
She drove on, head back, both wrists crossed on the
wheel. My square black hat crushed against the
roof, hands gripped between my knees, I listened,
helplessly, to Michael Jackson on station WVON,
then saw the silver hood nose into Chicago's squalid
Fifth Police District. What was this woman thinking? Were we stopping here? In this sewer? Wendy
parked beneath the last building on a side street.
Lincolns, Fleetwoods, El Dorados were everywhere.

Onto the sidewalk braying music spilled from an
old building—hundreds of years old—that looked
from below like a cinder block. I sucked in wind.
"You *live* here?"

She gave a quick hiss of laughter. "Are you
afraid?" Her eyes, small as nails, angled up to
mine.

"Yeah, I know you, Professor. We're really
'gods fallen into ruin,' right? Ain't that what you
said in class? Didn't you read that when you were
a lonely, fat little boy? And you wasted all those
years, learned twelve foreign languages, two of
them dead ones, you dimwit, wanting Great Sacrifices and trials of faith, believing you could con-
tribute to uplifting the Race—what else would a
fat boy dream of?—only to learn, too late, that
nobody wants your goddamn sacrifices. For all the
degrees and books, you're still a dork." Waving
her cigarette, she talked on like this, as if I had
been perfectly blind my whole life. "Civil rights is
high comedy. The old values are dead. Our money
is plastic. Our art is murder. Our philosophy is a
cackle, obscene and touching, from the tower. The
universe explodes silently nowhere, and you're dis-
turbed, you fossil, by decadent, erotic dreams,
lonely, hollowed out, nothing left now but the
Book—that boring ream of windy bullshit—you
can't finish." Her hair crackled suddenly with elec-
tricity. "Or maybe one last spiritless fuck, you
passéiste, with a student before you buy the farm.

Yeah," she said, opening her door, "I *know* you,
Professor."

I was too stunned to speak. If I'd known she
was this smart, I'd have given her an A the first
week of the term. Wendy pulled me, tripping, holding my head ducked a little, down cement steps into
a hallway of broken glass and garbage, then into a
long apartment so hazed with the raw, ugly scent
of marijuana hashish congolene and the damp smell
of old cellars that I could taste as well as smell these
violent odors as they coalesced, take hold of them
in my hands like tissue. For a moment I was dizzy.
Someone was sprawled dead drunk in the doorway.
Sound shook the air. The floorboards trembled.
Yet what most confounded me were the flashy men
in white mink jackets who favored women, the
women who looked, in this pale, fulgurating light,
like men. Meaning was in masquerade. I felt my
head going tighter. Let me linger too long and I
would never regain the university. Remembering
what she'd said, I felt tired, fat, and old. Damned
if I seduced her. Damned if I didn't. Ten, maybe
fifteen dancers, like dark chips of paint peeled from
the shadows, swept me from my briefcase and
Wendy. Someone pressed a pellet into my palm.
That scared me plenty. But what moved invisibly
in this hazy room, this hollow box of light, this
noise-curdled air, was more startling than the seen.
Music. It played hob with my blood pressure. It
was wild, sensual, clanging and languid by turns,

loud and liquid, an intangible force, or—what shall
I say?—spirit angling through the air, freed by
cackling instruments that lifted me, a fat boy and
student still, like a scrap of paper, then dropped
me, head over heels, into a dark corner by a man
or boy—I could not tell which—snorting white
powder off a dollar bill. He had a dragon tattooed
on his left arm, long braids like a Rastafarian, and
a face only a mother could love. Lapping up the
last of the powder, he gave me an underglance.
"What you lookin' at, chief?" "Nothing," I said.
"You gettin' high?" "No," I said. "You drinkin'?"
"No." "You *queer*?" "No!" "Then what the fuck
you doin' here?"

What had brought me here? Even I was no
longer sure what brought me. I became aware that
my palm was empty. *Lord*. My hand had brought
the pellet to my lips without telling my brain. *O
Lord*. Hours passed. Twice I tried to raise my arm,
but could not budge. Neither could I look away.
Silently, I watched. Helplessly, I accepted things
to smoke, sniff, and swallow—blotter acid Bud-
weiser raw ether Ripple. The room turned and
leaned. Slowly, a new prehension took hold of me,
echoing like a voice in my ear. That man, the one
in the Abo Po, lightly treading the measure, was
me. And this one dressed like Walt (or Joe) Fra-
zier was me. If I existed at all, it was in this ka-
leidoscopic party, this pinwheel of color, the I just
a function, a flickerflash creation of this black

chaos, the chaos no more, or less, than the *I*. There was an awful beauty in this. Seer and seen were intertwined—if you took the long view—in perpetuity. As it was, and apparently shall ever be, being sang being sang being in a cycle that was endless. I gazed, dizzily, back at the girl. She danced now fast, now slow. I followed her minutely as she moved. And then, perhaps I suffered hypnosis, or yet another hallucination, but my eyelids lowered, relaxing her afterimage into an explosion of energy, a light show in the blink, the pause before the world went black, and I suddenly saw Wendy—not as the girl who shotgunned me with blackmail back at Padelford Hall, who made me jump like a trained seal; who stood outside me as another subject in a contest of wills—but, yes, as pure light, brilliance, fluid like the music, blending in a perfectly balanced world with the players Muslims petty thieves black Jews lumpenproles Daley-machine politicians West Indians loungers Africans the drug peddlers who, when it came to the crunch, were, it was plain, pure light, too, the Whole in drag, and in that evanescent, drugged instant, I did indeed desperately love her.

Hours later, when I came out of this drug coma, the building was full of daylight, quiet, the loud party long past. Things, no longer hazed, had a stylized purity of line. Was there more to come? Was I done? I wondered if I had dreamed the connectedness of Being the night before, or if now, awake, I dreamed distinctions. I didn't know where I was for an instant. My bones felt loose, unlocked in my body. Through misty eyes I saw Wendy in an upholstered chair nearby, her arms around one brown knee, one bare foot on my briefcase, looking at me sadly, then away. I was twisted in covers on the mattress of a low bed, under a bare electric bulb, wearing only long flannel underwear limp from my sweat. Her bedroom was rayed by sunlight, cool as a basement. She sighed, a long stage sigh: "You poor fool." Her voice was flat and tired. "You're still thinking like a fat boy." She pulled off her blouse, her skirt, her other boot, and threw her cigarette still burning into a corner. As she lay down, her cold feet flat against me, I lifted my arm to let her move closer, and at last let my mind sleep.

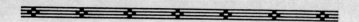

MOVING PICTURES

You sit in the Neptune Theater waiting for the thin, overhead lights to dim with a sense of respect, perhaps even reverence, for American movie houses are, as everyone knows, the new cathedrals, their stories better remembered than legends, totems, or mythologies, their directors more popular than novelists, more influential than saints—enough people, you've been told, have seen the James Bond adventures to fill the entire country of Argentina. Perhaps you have written this movie. Perhaps not. Regardless, you come to it as everyone does, as a seeker groping in the darkness for light, hoping something magical will be beamed from above, and no matter how bad this matinee is, or silly, something deep and maybe even too dangerous to talk loudly about will indeed happen to you and the others, before this drama reels to its last transparent frame.

Naturally, you have left your life outside the door. Like any life, it's a messy thing, hardly as orderly as art, what some call life in the fast lane: the Sanka and sugar-doughnut breakfasts, bumper-to-bumper traffic downtown, the business lunches, and a breakneck schedule not to get ahead but simply to stay in one place, which is peculiar, because you grew up in the sixties speeding on methadone and despising all this, knowing your Age (Aquarian) was made for finer stuff. But no matter. Outside, across town, you have put away for ninety minutes the tedious, repetitive job that is, obviously, beneath your talents, sensitivity, and education (a degree in English), the once beautiful woman—or wife—a former model (local), college dancer, or semiprofessional actress named Megan or Daphne, who has grown tired of you, or you of her, and talks now of legal separation and finding herself, the children from a former, frighteningly brief marriage whom you don't want to lose, the mortgage, alimony, IRS audit, the aging, gin-fattened face that once favored a rock star's but now frowns back at you in the bathroom mirror, the young woman at work born in 1960 and unable to recall John Kennedy who, after the Christmas party, took you to bed in her spacious downtown loft, perhaps out of pity because your mother, God bless her, died and left you with $1,000 in debt before you could get the old family house clear—all that shelved, mercifully, as the film starts, first that frosty mountaintop ringed by stars, or a lion roaring, or floodlights bathing the tips of buildings in a Hollywood skyline: stable trademarks in a world of flux, you think, surefire signs that whatever follows—tragedy or farce—is made by people who are accomplished dream merchants. Perhaps more: masters of vision, geniuses of the epistemological Murphy.

If you have written this film, which is possible, you look for your name in the credits, and probably frown at the names of the Crew, each recalling some disaster during the production, first at the studio, then later on location for five weeks in Oklahoma cow towns during the winter, which was worse than living on the moon, the days boiling and nights so cold. Nevertheless, you'd seen it as a miracle, an act of God when the director, having read your novel, called, offering you the project—a historical romance—then walked you patiently through the first eight drafts, suspicious of you at first (there was real money riding on this; it wasn't poetry), of your dreary, novelistic pretensions to Deep Profundity, and you equally suspicious of him, his background in sitcoms, obsession with "keeping it sexy," and love of Laurel and Hardy films. For this you wrote a dissertation on Derrida? Yet you'd listened. He was right, in the end.

He was good, you admitted, grudgingly. He knew,
as you—with your liberal arts degree—didn't, the
meaning of Entertainment. You'd learned. With
his help, you got good, too. You gloated. And lost
friends. "A movie?" said your poet friends. "That's
wonderful, it's happening for you," and then they
avoided you as if you had AIDS. What *was* happening was this:

You'd shelved the novel, the Big Book, for
bucks monitored by the Writers Guild (West),
threw yourself into fast-and-dirty scripts, the instant gratification of quick deadlines and fat checks
because the Book, with its complexity and promise
of critical praise, the Book, with its long-distance
demands and no financial reward whatsoever, was
impossible, and besides, you didn't have it anymore, not really, the gift for narrative or language,
while the scripts were easy, like writing shorthand,
and soon—way sooner than you thought—the films,
with their life span shorter than a mayfly's, were
all you could do. It's a living, you said. Nothing
lasts forever. And you pushed on.

The credits crawl up against a montage of
Oklahoma farm life, and in this you read a story,
too, even before the film begins. For the audience,
the actors are stars, the new Olympians, but oh,
you know them, this one—the male lead—whose
range is boundless, who could be a Brando, but who
hadn't seen work in two years before this role and
survived by doing voice-overs for a cartoon villain

in *The Smurfs*; that one—the female supporting role—who can play the full scale of emotions, but whose last memorable performance was a commercial for Rolaids, all of them; all, including you, fighting for life in a city where the air is so corrupt joggers spit black after a two-mile run; failing, trying desperately to keep up the front of doing-well, these actors, treating you shabbily sometimes because your salary was bigger than theirs, even larger than the producer's, though he wasn't exactly hurting—no, he was richer than a medieval king, a complex man of remarkable charm and cunning, someone both to admire for his Horatio Alger orphan-boy success and to fear for his worship at the altar of power. You won't forget the evening he asked you to his home after a long conference, served you scotch, and then, from inside a drawer in his desk removed an envelope, dumped its contents out, and you saw maybe fifty snapshots of beautiful, naked women on his bed—all of them second-rate actresses, though the female supporting role was there, too—and he watched you closely for your reaction, sipping his drink, smiling, then asked, "You ever sleep with a woman like that?" No, you hadn't. And no, you didn't trust him either. You didn't turn your back. But, then again, nobody in this business did, and in some ways he was, you knew, better than most.

You'd compromised, given up ground, won a few artistic points, but generally you agreed to the producer's ideas—it *was* his show—and then the small army of badly paid performers and production people took over, you trailing behind them in Oklahoma, trying to look writerly, wearing a Panama hat, holding your notepad ready for rewrites, surviving the tedium of eight or nine takes for difficult scenes, the fights, fallings-out, bad catered food, and midnight affairs, watching your script change at each level of interpretation—director, actor—until it was unrecognizable, a new thing entirely, a celebration of the Crew. Not you. Does anyone suspect how bad this thing really looked in rough cut? How miraculous it is that its rags of shots, conflicting ideas, and scraps of footage actually cohere? You sneak a look around at the audience, the faces lit by the glow of the screen. No one suspects. You've managed to fool them again, you old fox.

No matter whether the film is yours or not, it pulls you in, reels in your perception like a trout. On the narrow screen, the story begins with an establishing wide shot of an Oklahoma farm, then in close-up shows the face of a big, tow-headed, brown-freckled boy named Bret, and finally settles on a two-shot of Bret and his blond, bosomy girl friend, Bess. No margin for failure in a formula like that. In the opening funeral scene at a tiny whitewashed church, camera favors Bret, whose father has died. Our hero must seek his fortune in the city. Bess just hates to see him go. Dissolve to cemetery gate. As they leave the cemetery, and the coffin is lowered, she squeezes his hand, and something inside you shivers, the sense of ruin you felt at your own mother's funeral, the irreversible feeling of abandonment. There was no girl with you, but you wished to heaven there had been, the one named Sondra you knew in high school who wouldn't see you for squat, preferring basketball players to weird little wimps and geeks, which is pretty much what you were back then, a washout to those who knew you, but you give all that to Bret and Bess, the pain of parental loss, the hopeless, quiet love never to be, which thickens the screen so thoroughly that when Bess kisses Bret, your nose is clogged with tears and mucus, and then you have your handkerchief out, honking shamelessly, your eyes streaming, locked—even you—in a cycle of emotion (yours) which their images have borrowed, intensified, then given back to you, not because the images or sensations are sad, but because, at bottom, all you have known these last few minutes are the workings of your own nervous system. That is all you have ever known. You yourself have been supplying the grief and satisfaction all along, from within. But even that is not the true magic of film.

As Bret rides away, you remember sitting in the studio's tiny editing room amidst reels of film hanging like stockings in a bathroom, the editor, a fat, friendly man named Coates, tolerating your curiosity, letting you peer into his viewer as he patched the first reel together, figuring he owed you, a semifamous scriptwriter, that much. Each frame, you recall, was a single frozen image, like an individual thought, complete in itself, with no connection to the others, as if time stood still; but then the frames came faster as the viewer sped up, chasing each other, surging forward and creating a linear, continuous motion that outstripped your perception, and presto: a sensuously rich world erupted and took such nerve-knocking reality that you shielded your eyes when the harpsichord music came up and Bret stepped into a darkened Oklahoma shed seen only from his point of view—oh, yes, at times even your body responded, the sweat glands swaling, but it was lunchtime then and Coates wanted to go to the cafeteria for coffee and clicked off his viewer; the images flipped less quickly, slowed finally to a stop, the drama disappearing again into frames, and you saw, pulling on your coat, the nerve racking, heart-thumping vision for what it really was: the illusion of speed.

But is even that the magic of film? Sitting back in your seat, aware of your right leg falling asleep, you think so, for the film has no capacity to fool you anymore. You do not give it your feelings to transfigure. All that you see with godlike detachment are your own decisions, the lines that were dropped, and the microphone just visible in a corner of one scene. Nevertheless, it's gratifying to see the audience laugh out loud at the funny

parts, and blubber when Bret rides home at last to
marry Bess (actually, they hated each other on the
set), believing, as you can't, in a dream spun from
accelerated imagery. It almost makes a man feel
superior, like knowing how Uri Geller bends all
those spoons.

And then it is done, the theater emptying, the
hour and a half of illusion over. You file out with
the others, amazed by how so much can be projected
onto the tabula rasa of the Big Screen—grief, passion, fire, death—yet it remains, in the end, un-
touched. Dragging on your overcoat, the images
still an afterglow in your thoughts, you step outside to the street. It takes your eyes, still in low
gear, a moment to adjust to the light of late afternoon, traffic noise, and the things around you as
you walk to your Fiat, feeling good, the objects on
the street as flat and dimensionless at first as props
on a stage. And then you stop.

The Fiat, you notice, has been broken into.
The glove compartment has been rifled, and this
is where you keep a checkbook, an extra key to the
house, and where—you remember—you put the
report due tomorrow at nine sharp. The glove compartment, how does it look? Like a part of your
body, yes? A wound? From it spills a crumpled
photo of your wife, who has asked you to move out
so she can have the house, and another one of the
children, who haven't the faintest idea how empty
you feel getting up every morning to finance their

123

lives at a job that is a ghastly joke, given your talents, where you can't slow down and at least four competitors stand waiting for you to step aside, fall on your face, or die, and the injustice of all this, what you see in the narrow range of radiation you call vision, in the velocity of thought, is necessary and sufficient—as some logicians say—to bring your fists down again and again on the Fiat's roof. You climb inside, sit, furiously cranking the starter, then swear and lower your forehead to the steering wheel, which is, as anyone in Hollywood can tell you, conduct unbecoming a triple-threat talent like yourself: producer, star, and director in the longest, most fabulous show of all.

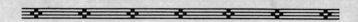

POPPER'S DISEASE

I.

I visit my patients frequently, particularly those on farms like Anna Montgomery. She's poor, as everyone knows, and lives with eleven cats in a dilapidated farmhouse near Murphysboro, too poor to pay my bills—that's true, except in molasses cookies, gossip about her children in Missouri, and hot cups of milk tea—but come winter, her roof buckles under the weight of snow, her plumbing freezes, and I dutifully make the long drive from Carbondale to dig a path to Anna's door, and check her cupboard, then her pulse.

Now, I do not mention these weekly visits to the poor to impress you, or to suggest that without Dr. Henry Popper's services these people would die (many problems, Lord knows, are beyond the pale of physics), but to explain how I came to be on a lonely country road after the severest snowstorm in the history of southern Illinois, and to assure you that, for all the crackpots who report unearthly phenomena, I am the most reliable of men.

House calls help my patients, obviously, but they help me, too. They take me away for hours. They take me, now that it's out in the open, away from my wife, Mildred. She's fifty, Swedish, still has her looks, and gives piano lessons to our paper boy, Gary Freeman—I think it's Gary this Sunday. He's fifteen, the son of Bob Freeman, our pharmacist and one of my friends. "You're only in the way," says Mildred, and I daresay she's right. She doesn't grudge my Saturday night poker games at the Court House with George Twenhafel, the mayor, and Judge Hal Withers, who started doing push-ups, against my advice, and had some sort of attack. They're white, I should add, and I'm not, except in the sense that perhaps *every*one these days in America is white, insofar as to ask, "Who am I?" is to ask, "By what social forces have I been shaped?" While logic would have it that I am Popper, perhaps you are Popper, too—or, more precisely, aren't we all tarred by the same cultural brush? Of course, Twenhafel, Withers, and I so cautiously avoid the topic of race during our get-togethers that the conversation seems to be about nothing but race. I'm not sure I understand them, and sometimes I'm convinced they don't understand me. Yet I have thought this puzzle through since my student days at Tuskegee, then Harvard, and it comforts me to believe we share the same cultural presuppositions—that history, for example, is linear, not circular, reason is preferable to emotion, and that one event "causes" another, although this is clearly, as many scientists have shown, an almost superstitious act of faith.

So my labor up frost-covered hills, alongside thick, unfenced woods, through cornfields bleached by snow gives Mildred and Gary a brief moment to practice "Für Elise," and gives me four hours to myself, my black medical bag beside me—dear old satchel of tricks, tools, all Western methodology in a portmanteau, my pipe crackling softly, and steamy car window parted slightly so I don't fall asleep. It is pleasant and quiet, out here on the road with the sky very blue, the wind cold, and the air clear. During these drives I pull hard on my pipe and ponder nothing as ordinary as my old woman's odd ways, but instead scientific problems that have puzzled me most of my life—the ontogenesis of personality, for example, which is fully explained by the famous French neurobiologist Henri Ey in *Études psychiatriques* (Vol. III, 1954). There can be little doubt that personality is the product—no—the historical creation of society. The world and man, according to Ey, engender one another, but this implied—and here my thoughts shift as quickly as gears on my Buick— that, ultimately, the most intimate features of a man's personality, those special aspects he believed individual and subjective and unique—kinks and quirks—had their origin, like Oxydol and doorknobs, in the public sphere, probably in pop culture. In other words, what we took to be essential in man throughout history might be accidental. A startling thesis, I'd have to say. But no more startling than the possibility that no man can escape the ceiling his culture sets for him, its special strengths and sicknesses. The case could be put in these terms: Certain aberrations in an Age might be so universal as to be unquestioned, and not recognized as problems for a thousand years. You'll think this mad, and I did, too, driving ten miles an hour, heavy snow swirling down; but I had been in half the sickrooms of southern Illinois, seen patients as physically healthy as prizefighters suddenly founder, then fail, and for no material reason, far as I could see, as if, strange to say, the malady lay in the invisible realm of values and belief.

Being an old man, I know theories are as plentiful as blackberries, so I'd be the last person to take such a playful hypothesis for true. These thoughts, however, kept my mind occupied during the drive to Anna Montgomery's. So occupied, in fact, that I was only faintly aware of the road sheering downhill, something streaking above the trees overhead, then static and a soft, miniature voice in my radio. The snow around me, it appeared, was melting. My foot shook on the accelerator. Then my engine got the hiccups, coughed, sputtered, and stopped cold. A shadow fell. Something blocked out the sun. The ground rumbled like eight-point-nine on the Richter scale, and I thought, *Earthquake*! They happen each spring in southern Illinois, but wasn't this winter? Cranking the starter key, slamming the stick into reverse, I saw through the frosty windshield—in a shock that made me whimper and rub my sleeve against the glass—a tremendous ship, two pie plates stuck together, hurtling soundlessly toward me, low, burning the crisp November air black with radiation. It zigzagged back and forth, snapping off a colonnade of tall-shafted pines atop a hill, then toppled Wayman Presley's fifty-foot cross (a local landmark of sorts) like a matchstick, made a hundred-degree turn without slowing down, then slogged into the earth. The explosion was stupendous, an earth-rocking blitz that ripped the roof off my car and threw me to one side of the road. Then all was quiet. For an instant I didn't know what it was hit me. My carhood was oxidized. My radiator boiled over. Faintly, the ship's relays and circuits clicked. Its surface burned first brick-red, then beryllium. And then something called to me from inside.

II.

You can well imagine the dread and despair this caused me. Flying saucers, I have read, were psychic phenomena, products of a troubled mind, particularly a mind broken by peering too long at the Abyss, but here before me in a field of brown slush, beneath a cindery sky, was a vessel the likes of which I'd never seen. (A complex ship powered by the synthesis of plutonium and ^4Yb, an ytterbium isotope. No time to relate this now. You'll find details elsewhere in this dossier.) That meant I was crazy. My mind had snapped—the result, I reasoned, of long hours at the hospital, too little sleep, talking cheerfully to patients only I knew would be dead before daybreak. What puzzled me was why lunacy had taken so long in coming. But crazy or not, I heard something squeal from inside. I was, as I say, still a physician. I picked up my bag, took two Pervitin, for I was still dazed, and forded weeds to the ship's entrance—a sort of orifice that opened with a quick, vegetable contraction as I came near. It looked real. It felt real. Quite possibly, it *was* real. Cautiously, I climbed inside. Behind me the hole closed with a hiss, a sphincteral snap so suggestive of the lower regions, of entombment, caskets and crypts that for a moment I could not move.

The wail grew louder. A shiver passed through my
back. If my intuition was right, this ship was older
than the world. The entrance blended into a maze
of propellant tanks, hatches, cables, crawl spaces:
a bathysphere, or so I thought at first. So far all
right.

But slowly the familiar blended into foreign
shapes as I patched on, pushing through walk-
ways smaller than those in a Civil War submarine.
The machinery I saw now (on the ceiling) favored glasswork sculpture, fantasmata that might
please the aesthetic taste of tarantulas. And it
didn't sound like machinery—it might have been
the echo of cell division I heard, the ring of enuclea-
tion, or embryo fission, the clack of hadrons col-
lapsing into their constituent quarks. Little as I
knew of space flight, I knew all technology was an
extension of the body, but here interior design did
not distinguish left (evil) or right (good), front
or back, as if the pilot had no center, physical or
metaphysical. What I felt was awe. What I felt,
plainly, was terror. Almost I wanted to flee. Nothing even vaguely human would build a vessel like
this. Now the wailing became a whimper. Then,
abruptly, all was light. There came a cool splash
of air, and I stood weaving in the lancet arch to a
new chamber. I drew my neck in. My palms began
to sweat, the way they perspired in the days when
I first dated Mildred, for as a young man in medical school, the only Negro in my class—the one

chosen to prove the Race's worth—I so doubted myself it seemed miraculous that a woman as beautiful as Mildred, with her light voice and brilliant eyes, would have me. Success in middle age, even the citations on my office wall, had not shaken this feeling that I'd not fully comprehended my own (foster) culture, that George Twenhafel, who counted it as his heritage, understood something I did not. Why these thoughts arose as I groped deeper into the saucer, I cannot say. Its strangeness seemed to trigger in me the same primordial feeling of *thrownness* that every Negro experiences when hurled into a society that simultaneously supports and, I am saying, annihilates him, because he can find reflections of himself nowhere in it—like a falcon exiled, say, to the Lifeworld of fish, always off-balance, but finally embracing the alien in all its otherness, yet never sure if he's got it right. (My ancestors—or so I've read—had a hundred concepts for the African community, but none for the "individual," who, as we define him today—the lonely Leibnizean monad—is an invention of the Industrial Age, as romantic love is the product of medieval poets. My ancestors, I've also heard, were pre-Industrial and, therefore, are no test of reality. But enough.) Panting a little now, I stepped inside, pouring sweat. . . .

Well, no point in B-movie melodrama.

The Creature was hideous beyond belief, but there's no reason to bang the harpsichord about it.

To any man who saw him, it would seem he was a huge boiled crayfish about the size of a fence post, sprinkled with a little squid, lobster, and jumbo shrimp—what you might expect to find on a seafood platter in a decent restaurant, or on the pages of *Planet Stories*. Whenever he moved, he left a trail of paste or organic matter. I stayed a respectful distance from this vision, who (I learned later) had six claws, eighty-four teeth, three antennae, two stomachs like a cow, and four enormous tentacles—his, he told me, later, was a family for large tentacles, which I believed. What else could I say? I knew nothing of his standards for beauty and truth, or even if he *had* such standards. And what did his control room contain? Spectrometers, I guess. Particle detectors. The only furnishings were four-feet-high platforms on the floor. In their bases lights were recessed. A wall-to-wall Telecipher—a sort of electronic speculum, with a screen thin as hair and integrated circuitry—processed data from Carbondale, Benton, Herrin, and Elkville. It could multiply, divide, add, do square and cubic roots, Boolean equations, calculate in metalanguage, or the Hilbert-Ackermann system, or deploy Rs_1 logical strategies, and I couldn't for the life of me guess its full capabilities. Even so, a physician knows an unhealthy being when he sees one. Entering the room, putting away my knife, I could tell the pilot wasn't exactly running on all twelve cylinders. He gave a Dostoyevskian sigh.

He looked sick as mud. What convinced me of his sensitivity, however, was that he had a Cambridge manner, and the pallor any creature has when he is trying to ask directions in German.

"No—speak English." I placed my bag on a platform by the Telecipher. "Speak English. You have landed in America. Are you injured?" I felt, rather than heard, the Creature say, "Quite." Telegnosis. What English he knew, as it turned out, came from eavesdropping on radio broadcasts around Cambridge and Amherst College— he pronounced *car* as "cah" and *water* came out as "waddah," which diminished his strangeness by a little. When introductions were over and he had taken my coat and politely offered me a part of the floor to eat (the whole saucer was edible, a fifty-four-thousand-ton Hershey bar), he touched the outside of my elbows as he talked, taking both my hands in his tentacles, and confessed in a very apologetic voice, "I don't want you to get the wrong idea. I'm not a Big Noise on my world, Henry. I am what you call a carrier. I have been quarantined."

"Quarantined, you say?" I withdrew my pipe and charged it. "You're not an ambassador or a diplomat?"

"No, I'm afraid not. On my world I'm the equivalent of your street people—I'm not even sure how this ship works. I'm sorry."

"Then why were you sent here?"

"They can't cure me," he said. "They use Earth as a leper colony."

This was all very unsatisfying. All these centuries we'd hoped for higher technology, wisdom. And what tumbled down from space? *Outpatients.* I sighed, tamping my pipe down with my thumb. "You want our medical opinion?"

"Now you understand. On my world the sickness is called by various names, but none as accurate as 'the Plague.' What I mean to say, Dr. Popper, Henry—may I call you Henry?—is that I have been exiled until either this disease passes or your culture discovers a remedy. Your research in this area skyrocketed in Vienna in 1884, Göttingen in 1916, then at Duquesne, Stony Brook, and Northwestern ten years ago. Don't be alarmed. It's not contagious. The Plague is not a disorder of your world, to my knowledge. It can't be passed physically, or picked up by sitting on toilet seats at the Trailways station."

"Of course." I smiled, just faintly, frightened, and took another step back. I couldn't shake the urge to spread tartar sauce on him. "Can you tell me the symptoms?"

"Well," he said, touching the tips of his tentacles, looking away, "for no apparent reason, and without the slightest warning, I experience feelings of first a tightness in the cerebral area, a tremor or unpleasant quiver, then a shock of dislocation, cold sweat, followed by vomiting, vertigo—the sense of falling, the inability to ascertain precisely what things mean, and the peculiar sense that I am somehow dependent upon everything in my perceptual field: *xlanthia*, *hbeds*, or *sploks*, which have a curious opacity, a marvelous beauty"—here he burst into tears—"yet threaten to absorb me, engulf me, annihilate me completely, because I am, in a word, deeply and inexorably *different* from them." His anguish exploded in my mind. "It's nauseating, do you see?"

"Steady there." I reached to pat his shoulder or knee—it was hard to tell which. "You don't have to go on." The effort to explain had greatly excited him—he was smoking. He stared, blankly, like a shock victim. Gambling, I gave him Trional. "Just tell me how to get out and I'll bring help—"

"So," he said, cutting me off, five tentacles slithering over what might have been a wet forehead, "so I feel a horrified fascination for the *sploks* and so desire (and yet dread) them that I yearn for their recognition, shift from melancholy to euphoria, and think of nothing else, which"—his voice quavered—"has led other Plague victims to irascibility, violence, moodiness, a morbid fascination with Time, boredom, the loss of memory, and, worst of all, thermogenesis."

"Beg pardon?" I asked. "Thermogenesis?"

138

"It's what you call internal combustion. The Plague affects us that way, physically. The final stage is extinction. We explode."

"When you say explode, do you mean *explode*?"

"Like Chinese fireworks," he said. "Like an MTV music-video."

"Horrible!" I swallowed. Then: "Did I come in through that corridor or—"

"You haven't heard the worst." His voice was frail. "I can thermogenerate at any moment."

I gave the Creature a dose of diphenylhydantoin.

It's not every day a Negro doctor is delivered a new medical anomaly with, as it were, a red ribbon around it. It was, accordingly, as you see, an awful affliction. *Awful!* He now stood only as high as my chest. The room was full of smoke. Psychosomatic, I'd have to say, and how it might be cured was more than I could have told you, but a man who has survived Carbondale for thirty years is an eternal optimist. We had but to isolate the cause of the Plague to name it, but name it to know its nature. The Nobel Prize would be a *gift* to whoever diagnosed, then cured this uncanny disease. It was front-page stuff. Medical history, I hoped, might even rename it after me. Realizing I would need help for a real examination, I fumbled into my coat, and hurried to the Telecipher for my bag. It was then that, looking up, I saw—or thought I saw—a man with a crowbar crack the lock to a farmhouse full of cats, enter, which startled an old woman inside, then smash her head like a melon. Was this Anna? As he tore at her dress, there was a break in the film, some markings, then I saw another woman, younger, and quietly eagle-rocking her hips under a boy on a high bed with a carved oak headboard. She wore a pink slip like the one I had bought last year at Penney's for Mildred. Peering at the screen, I saw . . .

"That's my wife!" I croaked. "Can you turn this thing up?"

The Creature increased the volume. "Would you like the odors, too? This device, as far as I understand it . . ."

I missed whatever he said next, for now I heard the suction of sweating bodies, whiffed the venereal, fishlike bouquet of love. My old woman sighed, "Oh, Doctor . . ." I leaned forward, sweating from the soles of my feet upward, fingers in my beard; then, in disbelief, I saw Gary Freeman, his back glistening with perspiration, pull on a pair of Danger High Voltage slacks, and dry Mildred with one of my best Hawaiian shirts. Chuckling, he held it up to his face. "Does Henry really wear this shit?" My stomach tightened. My throat squeezed as if in a fist. On Mildred's walnut bureau, a crumpled Trojan lay atop a copy of *The Joy of Classical Piano*. I closed my eyes, counted twenty, turned my face from the screen, then opened my lids quickly. They fell to it again. They shook my picture off the wall.

"You're the only medicine I need," groaned Mildred.

I had cardiac arrest for the rest of my life. Too weak to stand, I sat heavily on the platform, opened my bag, took out the sphygmometer, and checked my blood pressure: 140 over 110.

The Creature gently placed a tentacle on my shoulder. "Come away, Henry." He adjusted the Telecipher—"It seems we are both strangers here, no?"—which responded by flashing from my bedroom to images of his Lifeworld—a low-gravity planet in the Alpha Centauri-A galaxy, a star system much like our own—but I was too shaken to pay attention. I pulled loose my collar. How in heaven's name could she *do* this to me? Trembling, I gave myself a shot of Dilantin and closed my eyes. They were right, Gary and Mildred; I was wrong. You couldn't really fault Mildred or the boy if, as the new morality said, a man like me, an antique Negro with my close-cropped haircut, heavy glasses that diffused my pupils, Murray's hair pomade, and funny Old Testament ways, was a relic—the product of ideas obsolete before I was born. By the way the world reckoned things, I was, at fifty-eight, Victorian, out of fuel now and running on the fumes. Old and crapped out. A pain corkscrewed through my chest. Should I weep? Should I call my attorney? Should I return to the only thing in this world that gave my life ballast: my work? I wheeled away, still flushed with confusion, from the Telecipher with this in mind, only to discover that the Creature had in my moment of confusion gone critical and was now so sensitive and over-wrought that the slightest contact with objects in the saucer made him wince. "I want to say God bless you, Henry, and thank you for trying." He smiled sickly at me. He was no taller than my knee. His mouth slipped sideways, then he fell, his figure forming an X that seemed to obliterate everything. "The idea has just occurred to me that all phenomena are products of my ego."

Poor creature, he was past helping.

"You have to tell me how to get out." I lifted his head; it fell back, heavy and soft, like a bag. "Do you know how the door opens?"

Evidently, he did not know.

"I'm not Schweitzer!" I said. "Where's the key?"

In the terror of seeing him die instantly, the explosion going through me like a shock, and in the terror of being certain that without the Creature I was trapped, I backed away, then toward him, my terror greatest of all when I found no Creature there, merely vapor spiraling from a pool of black serum.

"I'm not Christiaan Barnard!" I whispered, hoping, perhaps, the words would, as in a dream dissolving, bring me back to my Buick. My eyes were swimming. My cry ricocheted about the chamber. Then the Telecipher, still beaconing, showed a thing so unearthly, so spectral my mouth fell open and I dropped my bag.

III.

My patient expired November 24. The flying saucer, predictably, has been quarantined by the army in the cornfield where it fell. They're afraid, it's clear, of a biological crisis, afraid to use cutting torches until I tell them the situation inside. It's March, by my guess, or April—the snow in southern Illinois has vanished, but the winter chill remains locked in the strange metal of the ship's corridors, which I walk and walk when not reviewing the Telecipher's endless memory tubes for some clue that will open the exit. My labor is endless. The machine at times seems to contain my mind. The entries are infinite, ton upon ton of empirical data on every subject between the Milky Way and Alpha Centauri-A. On its keyboard you can play infinite variations on knowledge. It teaches me what questions to ask. It teaches me patience. Slowly, I progress. Quietly, I program the machine for answers, probability, analysis. My patient was, I know, old: millions of years old, and once I thought I'd unkeyed the cause of his affliction. It was partly this fact that so frightened me last winter: Their cities with fragile buildings like works of glass,

143

where bridges seemed to flow as fluidly as the water beneath them, were full of shocks and mysteries, a glimpse into the ineffable Yonder—cities of such beauty and antiquity that centuries before *Pithecanthropus* (Peking Man) these creatures founded their metaphysic foursquare on what we would call, roughly, a theory of quantum electrodynamics. In their culture, Dualism was death. The whole picture came slowly, like a collage, piece by piece, the Telecipher scolding me for my failure to grasp it instantly. For what it's worth, I will explain this odd Lifeworld, though I hardly understood two images in three on the screen, and do not trust my diagnosis.

In what may or may not have been a wise experiment, I programmed the Telecipher to interface relativity and what I recalled from Ey's elegant series of papers on neurobiology, and it read UNCODABLE QUESTION STUPID, then reconsidered, recircuited the data, and said this about the Creature's science: a quantum field, as they understood it, was the vast laboratory of subatomic phenomena in which quanta of energy simultaneously took form as particles ($A=A$) and waves ($A=not-A$). As such, the field dissolved the distinction between solid particles and the space surrounding them. (Don't get impatient—I'm coming to the point.) Continuous in time, everywhere in space, the field was the idea of polymorphy made fact, its particles mere concretions of energy, as if Being delighted in playing hide-and-seek with itself, dressing up, so to speak, as Everything, then sloughed off particularities when bored with the game. Remarkably, the Telecipher then proceeded to diagnose the Plague. Dear God, I thought. It can't be true. My mind rejected it immediately. The margin of error seemed too great; I must have misread the evidence. I reran the tapes, then headed for the entrance, squeezing my hands together, my heart still racing after what I'd seen.

From outside I first heard Mildred, then George Twenhafel shouting, "Hen-*ry!*" I placed my stethoscope against the door to hear them better, and heard the mayor bark, "Popper, what are you *doing* in there? Are they dead?" Mildred wept with wronged nobility. "He's *never* done anything like this before." There were other voices, a flurry of talk about a press blackout, a possible epidemic from Mars; then Twenhafel's voice came back, gentler, conciliatory, like a father coaxing his child down from a tree: "If you're sick, we can help you, Henry, but the hospital needs something to go on."

Any physician who wishes to be taken seriously, especially a Negro doctor, must swear by his diagnosis. He must be compassionate, too. Because you cannot tell the terminal patient he has but a week to live, I hesitated. My throat was dry. I whispered, "George——"

"Yes, Henry. What killed them?"

"The machine said——" I paused, certain I'd

programmed the Creature's machine incorrectly. In the control room's wizardly light, very blue, and not an angstrom from the smoldering remains of the pilot, whose world until now had believed thought and things to be of the same species, in a brilliant readout like my own mind stammering, I had seen the screen, had seen it clearly and definitely fulgurate like lightning in a few fibrous seconds *It's the Self* and *There is no cure*

THE SORCERER'S
APPRENTICE

There was a time, long ago, when many sorcerers lived in South Carolina, men not long from slavery who remembered the white magic of the Ekpe Cults and Cameroons, and by far the greatest of these wizards was a blacksmith named Rubin Bailey. Believing he was old, and would soon die, the Sorcerer decided to pass his learning along to an apprentice. From a family near Abbeville he selected a boy, Allan, whose father, Richard Jackson, Rubin once healed after an accident, and for this Allan loved the Sorcerer, especially the effects of his craft, which comforted the sick, held back evil, and blighted the enemies of newly freed slaves with locusts and bad health. "My house," Richard told the wizard, "has been honored." His son swore to

serve his teacher faithfully, then those who looked
to the Sorcerer, in all ways. With his father's bless-
ing, the boy moved his belongings into the Sorcerer's home, a houseboat covered with strips of
scrapmetal, on the river.

But Rubin Bailey's first teachings seemed
to Allan to be no teachings at all. "Bring in fresh
water," Rubin told his apprentice. "Scrape barna-
cles off the boat." He never spoke of sorcery.
Around the boy he tied his blacksmith's apron, and
guided his hand in hammering out the horseshoes
Rubin sold in town, but not once in the first month
did Rubin pass along the recipes for magic. Patiently, Allan performed these duties in perfect
submission to the Sorcerer, for it seemed rude to
express displeasure to a man he wished to emulate,
but his heart knocked for the higher knowledge,
the techniques that would, he hoped, work miracles.

At last, as they finished a meal of boiled pork
and collards one evening, he complained bitterly:
"You haven't told me anything yet!" Allan re-
gretted this outburst immediately, and lowered his
head. "Have I done wrong?"

For a moment the Sorcerer was silent. He
spiced his coffee with rum, dipped in his bread,
chewed slowly, then looked up, steadily, at the boy.
"You are the best of students. And you wish to do
good, but you can't be too faithful, or too eager,
or the good becomes evil."

"Now I don't understand," Allan said. "By

themselves the tricks aren't good *or* evil, and if you plan to do good, then the results must be good."

Rubin exhaled, finished his coffee, then shoved his plate toward the boy. "Clean the dishes," he said. Then, more gently: "What I know has worked I will teach. There is no certainty these things can work for you, or even for me, a second time. White magic comes and goes. I'm teaching you a trade, Allan. You will never starve. This is because after fifty years, I still can't foresee if an incantation will be magic or foolishness."

These were not, of course, the answers Allan longed to hear. He said, "Yes, sir," and quietly cleared away their dishes. If he had replied aloud to Rubin, as he did silently while toweling dry their silverware later that night, he would have told the Sorcerer, "You are the greatest magician in the world because you have studied magic and the long-dead masters of magic, and I believe, even if you do not, that the secret of doing good is a good heart and having a hundred spells at your disposal, so I will study everything—the words and timbre and tone of your voice as you conjure, and listen to those you have heard. Then I, too, will have magic and can do good." He washed his underwear in the moonlight, as is fitting for a fledgling magician, tossed his dishpan water into the river, and, after hanging his washpail on a hook behind Rubin's front door, undressed, and fell asleep with these thoughts: To do good is a very

great thing, the *only* thing, but a magician must
be able to conjure at a moment's notice. Surely it
is all a question of know-how.

So it was that after a few months the Sorcerer's apprentice learned well and quickly when
Rubin Bailey finally began to teach. In Allan's
growth was the greatest joy. Each spell he showed
proudly to his father and Richard's friends when
he traveled home once a year. Unbeknownst to the
Sorcerer, he held simple exhibits for their entertainment—harmless prestidigitation like throwing
his voice or levitating logs stacked by the toolshed.
However pleased Richard might have been, he gave
no sign. Allan's father never joked or laughed too
loudly. He was the sort of man who held his feelings in, and people took this for strength. Allan's
mother, Beatrice, a tall, thick-waisted woman, had
told him (for Richard would not) how when she
was carrying Allan, they rode a haywagon to a
scrub-ball in Abbeville on Freedom Day. Richard
fell beneath the wagon. A wheel smashed his thumb
open to the bone. "Somebody better go for Rubin
Bailey," was all Richard said, and he stared like
it might be a stranger's hand. And Allan remembered Richard toiling so long in the sun he couldn't
eat some evenings unless he first emptied his stomach by forcing himself to vomit. His father squir-
reled away money in their mattresses, saving for
seven years to buy the land they worked. When he
had $600—half what they needed—he grew afraid

of theft, so Beatrice took their money to one of the banks in town. She stood in line behind a northern-looking Negro who said his name was Grady Armstrong. "I work for the bank across the street," he told Beatrice. "You wouldn't be interested in part-time work, would you? We need a woman to clean, someone reliable, but she has to keep her savings with us." Didn't they need the money? Beatrice would ask Allan, later, when Richard left them alone at night. Wouldn't the extra work help her husband? She followed Grady Armstrong, whose easy, loose-hinged walk led them to the second bank across the street. "Have you ever deposited money before?" asked Grady. "No," she said. Taking her envelope, he said, "Then I'll do it for you." On the boardwalk, Beatrice waited. And waited. After five minutes, she opened the door, found no Grady Armstrong, and flew screaming the fifteen miles back to the fields and Richard, who listened and chewed his lip, but said nothing. He leaned, Allan remembered, in the farmhouse door, smoking his cigars and watching only Lord knew what in the darkness—exactly as he stood the following year, when Beatrice, after swallowing rat poison, passed on.

Allan supposed it was risky to feel if you had grown up, like Richard, in a world of nightriders. There was too much to lose. Any attachment ended in separation, grief. If once you let yourself care, the crying might never stop. So he assumed his father was pleased with his apprenticeship to Rubin, though hearing him say this would have meant the world to Allan. He did not mind that somehow the Sorcerer's personality seemed to permeate each spell like sweat staining fresh wood, because this, too, seemed to be the way of things. The magic was Rubin Bailey's, but when pressed, the Sorcerer confessed that the spells had been in circulation for centuries. They were a web of history and culture, like the king-sized quilts you saw as curiosities at country fairs, sewn by every woman in Abbeville, each having finished only a section, a single flower perhaps, so no man, strictly speaking, could own a mystic spell. "But when you kill a bird by pointing," crabbed Rubin from his rocking chair, "you don't *haveta* wave your left hand in the air and pinch your forefinger and thumb together like I do."

"Did I do that?" asked Allan.

Rubin hawked and spit over the side of the houseboat. "Every time."

"I just wanted to get it right." Looking at his hand, he felt ashamed—he was, after all, right-handed—then shoved it deep into his breeches. "The way you do it is so beautiful."

"I know." Rubin laughed. He reached into his coat, brought out his pipe, and looked for matches. Allan stepped inside, and the Sorcerer shouted behind him, "You shouldn't do it because my own

154

teacher, who wore out fifteen flying carpets in his lifetime, told me it was wrong."

"Wrong?" The boy returned. He held a match close to the bowl of Rubin's pipe, cupping the flame. "Then why do you do it?"

"It works best for me that way, Allan. I have arthritis." He slanted his eyes left at his pupil. "Do you?"

The years passed, and Allan improved, even showing a certain flair, a style all his own that pleased Rubin, who praised the boy for his native talent, which did not come from knowledge and, it struck Allan, was wholly unreliable. When Esther Peters, a seamstress, broke her hip, it was not Rubin who the old woman called, but young Allan, who sat stiffly on a fiddle-back chair by her pallet, the fingers of his left hand spread over the bony ledge of her brow and rheumy eyes, whispering the rune that lifted her pain after Esther stopped asking, "Does he know what he doing, Rubin? This ain't how you did when I caught my hand in that cotton gin." Afterwards, as they walked the dark footpath leading back to the river, Rubin in front, the Sorcerer shared a fifth with the boy and paid him a terrifying compliment: "That was the best I've seen anybody do the spell for exorcism." He stroked his pupil's head. "God took *holt* of you back there—I don't see how you can do it that good again." The smile at the corners of Allan's mouth weighed a ton. He handed back Rubin's bottle, and said, "Me neither." The Sorcerer's flattery, if this was flattery, suspiciously resembled Halloween candy with hemlock inside. Allan could not speak to Rubin the rest of that night.

In the old days of sorcery, it often happened that pupils came to mistrust most their finest creations, those frighteningly effortless works that flew mysteriously from their lips when they weren't looking, and left the apprentice feeling, despite his pride, as baffled as his audience and afraid for his future—this was most true when the compliments compared a fledgling wizard to other magicians, as if the apprentice had achieved nothing new, or on his own. This is how Allan felt. The charm that cured Esther had whipped through him like wind through a reedpipe, or—more exactly, like music struggling to break free, liberate its volume and immensity from the confines of wood and brass. It made him feel unessential, anonymous, like a tool in which the spell sang itself, briefly borrowing his throat, then tossed him, Allan, aside when the miracle ended. To be so used was thrilling, but it gave the boy many bad nights. He lay half on his bed, half off. While Rubin slept, he yanked on his breeches and slipped outside. The river trembled with moonlight. Not far away, in a rowboat, a young man unbuttoned his lover. Allan heard their laughter and fought down the loneliness of a life devoted to discipline and sorcery. So many sacrifices.

So many hours spent hunched over yellow, worm-holed scrolls. He pitched small pebbles into the water, and thought, If a conjurer cannot conjure at will, he is worthless. He must have knowledge, an armory of techniques, a thousand strategies, if he is to unfailingly do good. Toward this end the apprentice applied himself, often despising the spontaneity of his first achievement. He watched Rubin Bailey closely until on his fifth year on the river he had stayed by the Sorcerer too long and there was no more to learn.

"That can't be," said Allan. He was twenty-five, a full sorcerer himself by most standards, very handsome, more like his father now, at the height of his technical powers, with many honors and much brilliant thaumaturgy behind him, though none half as satisfying as his first exorcism rune for Esther Peters. He had, generally, the respect of everyone in Abbeville. And, it must be said, they waited eagerly for word of his first solo demonstration. This tortured Allan. He paced around the table, where Rubin sat repairing a fishing line. His belongings, rolled in a blanket, lay by the door. He pleaded, "There must be *one* more strategy."

"One more maybe," agreed the Sorcerer. "But what you need to know, you'll learn."

"Without you?" Allan shuddered. He saw himself, in a flash of probable futures, failing Rubin. Dishonoring Richard. Ridiculed by everyone. "How *can* I learn without you?"

"You just do like you did that evening when you helped Esther Peters. . . ."

That wasn't me, thought Allan. I was younger. I don't know how, but everything worked then. You were behind me. I've tried. I've tried the rain-making charm over and over. *It doesn't rain!* They're only words!

The old Sorcerer stood up and embraced Allan quickly, for he did not like sloppy good-byes or lingering glances or the silly things people said when they had to get across a room and out the door. "You go home and wait for your first caller. You'll do fine."

Allan followed his bare feet away from the houseboat, his head lowered and a light pain in his chest, a sort of flutter like a pigeon beating its wings over his heart—an old pain that first began when he suspected that pansophical knowledge counted for nothing. The apprentice said the spell for fair weather. Fifteen minutes later a light rain fell. He traipsed through mud into Abbeville, shoved his bag under an empty table in a tavern, and sat dripping in the shadows until he dried. A fat man pounded an off-key piano. Boot heels stamped the floor beneath Allan, who ordered te-quila. He sucked lemon slices and drained off shot glasses. Gradually, liquor backwashed in his throat and the ache disappeared and his body felt trans-parent. Yet still he wondered: Was sorcery a gift given to a few, like poetry? Did the Lord come, lift

you up, then drop you forever? If so, then he was
finished, bottomed out, bellied up before he even began. He had not been born among the Allmuseri
Tribe in Africa, like Rubin, if this was necessary
for magic. He had not come to New Orleans in a
slave clipper, or been sold at the Cabildo, if this
was necessary. He had only, it seemed, a vast and
painfully acquired yet hollow repertoire of tricks,
and this meant he could be a parlor magician, which
paid well enough, but he would never do good. If
he could not help, what then? He knew no other
trade. He had no other dignity. He had no other
means to transform the world and no other influ-
ence upon men. His seventh tequila untasted, Allan
squeezed the bridge of his nose with two fingers,
rummaging through his mind for Rubin's phrase
for the transmogrification of liquids into vapor.
The demons of drunkenness (Saphathoral) and
slow-thinking (Ruax) tangled his thoughts, but
finally the words floated topside. Softly, he spoke
the phrase, stunned at its beauty—at the Sorcerer's
beauty, really—mumbling it under his breath so
no one might hear, then opened his eyes on the soaking, square face of a man who wore a blue homespun
shirt and butternut trousers, but had not been there
an instant before: his father. Maybe he'd said the
phrase for telekinesis. "Allan, I've been looking all
over. How are you?"

"Like you see." His gaze dropped from his
father to the full shot glass and he despaired.

"Are you sure you're all right? Your eyelids are puffy."

"I'm okay." He lifted the shot glass and made its contents vanish naturally. "I've had my last lesson."

"I know—I went looking for you on the river, and Rubin said you'd come home. Since I knew better, I came to Abbeville. There's a girl at the house wants to see you—Lizzie Harris. She was there when you sawed Deacon Wills in half." Richard picked up his son's bag. "She wants you to help her to—"

Allan shook his head violently. "Lizzie should see Rubin."

"She has." He reached for Allan's hat and placed it on his son's head. "He sent her to you. She's been waiting for hours."

Much rain fell upon Allan and his father, who walked as if his feet hurt, as they left town, but mainly it fell on Allan. His father's confidence in him was painful, his chatter about his son's promising future like the chronicle of someone else's life. This was the night that was bound to come. And now, he thought as they neared the tiny, hip-roofed farmhouse, swimming in fog, I shall fall from humiliation to impotency, from impotency to failure, from failure to death. He leaned weakly against the porch rail. His father scrambled ahead of him, though he was a big man built for endurance and not for speed, and stepped back to open the door

for Allan. The Sorcerer's apprentice, stepping inside, decided quietly, definitely, without hope that
if this solo flight failed, he would work upon himself
the one spell Rubin had described but dared not
demonstrate. If he could not help this girl Lizzie—
and he feared he could not—he would go back to the
river and bring forth demons—horrors that broke
a man in half, ate his soul, then dragged him below
the ground, where, Allan decided, those who could
not do well the work of a magician belonged.

"Allan's here," his father said to someone in
the sitting room. "My son is a Conjure Doctor, you
know."

"I seen him," said a girl's voice. "Looks like
he knows everything there is to know about magic."

The house, full of heirlooms, had changed little since Allan's last year with Rubin. The furniture was darkened by use. All the mirrors in his
mother's bedroom were still covered by cloth. His
father left week-old dishes on the hob, footswept
his cigars under the bare, loose floorboards, and
paint on the front porch had begun to peel in large
strips. There in the sitting room, Lizzie Harris sat
on Beatrice's old flat-bottomed roundabout. She
was twice as big as Allan remembered her. Her loose
dress and breast exposed as she fed her baby made,
he supposed, the difference. Allan looked away while
Lizzie drew her dress up, then reached into her bead
purse for a shinplaster—Civil War currency—
which she handed to him. "This is all you have?" He

returned her money, pulled a milk stool beside her, and said, "Please, sit down." His hands were trembling. He needed to hold something to hide the shaking. Allan squeezed both his knees. "Now," he said, "what's wrong with the child?"

"Pearl don't eat," said Lizzie. "She hasn't touched food in two days, and the medicine Dr. Britton give her makes her spit. It's a simple thing," the girl assured him. "Make her eat."

He lifted the baby off Lizzie's lap, pulling the covering from her face. That she was beautiful made his hands shake even more. She kept her fists balled at her cheeks. Her eyes were light, bread-colored, but latticed by blood vessels. Allan said to his father, without facing him, "I think I need boiled Hound's Tongue and Sage. They're in my bag. Bring me the water from the herbs in a bowl." He hoisted the baby higher on his right arm and, holding the spoon of cold cereal in his left hand, praying silently, began a litany of every spell he knew to disperse suffering and the afflictions of the spirit. From his memory, where techniques lay stacked like crates in a storage bin, Allan unleashed a salvo of incantations. His father, standing nearby with a discolored spoon and the bowl, held his breath so long Allan could hear flies gently beating against the lamp glass of the lantern. Allan, using the spoon like a horseshoe, slipped the potion between her lips. "Eat, Pearl," the apprentice whis-

pered. "Eat and live." Pearl spit up on his shirt.
Allan closed his eyes and repeated slowly every syl-
lable of every word of every spell in his possession.
And ever he pushed the spoon of cereal against the
child's teeth, ever she pushed it away, gagging,
swinging her head, and wailing so Allan had to
shout each word above her voice. He oozed sweat
now. Wind changing direction outside shifted the
pressure inside the room so suddenly that Allan's
stomach turned violently—it was if the farmhouse,
snatched up a thousand feet, now hung in space.
Pearl spit first clear fluids. Then blood. The apprentice attacked this mystery with a dazzling ar-
ray of devices, analyzed it, looked at her with the
critical, wrinkled brow of a philosopher, and mimed
the Sorcerer so perfectly it seemed that Rubin, not
Allan, worked magic in the room. But he was not
Rubin Bailey. And the child suddenly stopped its
struggle and relaxed in the apprentice's arms.

Lizzie yelped, "Why ain't Pearl crying?" He
began repeating, futilely, his spells for the fifth
time. Lizzie snatched his arm with such strength
her fingers left blue spots on his skin. "That's
enough!" she said. "You give her to me!"

"There's another way," Allan said, "another
charm I've seen." But Lizzie Harris had reached
the door. She threw a brusque "Good-bye" behind
her to Richard and nothing to Allan. He knew they
were back on the ground when Lizzie disappeared

163

outside. Within the hour she would be at Rubin's houseboat. In two hours she would be at Esther Peters's home, broadcasting his failure.

"Allan," said Richard, stunned. "It didn't work."

"It's never worked." Allan put away the bowl, looked around the farmhouse for his bag, then a pail, and kissed his father's rough cheek. Startled, Richard pulled back sharply, as if he had stumbled sideways against the kiln. "I'm sorry," said Allan. It was not an easy thing to touch a man who so guarded, and for good reason, his emotions. "I'm not much of a Sorcerer, or blacksmith, or anything else."

"You're not going out this late, are you?" His father struggled, and Allan felt guilty for further confusing him with feeling. "Allan. . . ."

His voice trailed off.

"There's one last spell I have to do." Allan touched his arm lightly, once, then drew back his hand. "Don't follow me, okay?"

On his way to the river Allan gathered the roots and stalks and stones he required to dredge up the demon kings. The sky was clear, the air dense, and the Devil was in it if he fouled even this conjuration. For now he was sure that white magic did not reside in ratiocination, education, or will. Skill was of no service. His talent was for pa(o)stiche. He could imitate but never truly heal;

impress but never conjure beauty; ape the good
but never again give rise to a genuine spell. For
that God or Creation, or the universe—it had sev-
eral names—had to seize you, *use* you, as the Sorcerer said, because it needed a womb, shake you
down, speak through you until the pain pearled
into a beautiful spell that snapped the world back
together. It had abandoned Allan, this possession.
It had taken him, in a way, like a lover, planted one
pitiful seed, and said, " 'Bye now." This absence,
this emptiness, this sterility he felt deep at his center. Beyond all doubt, he owed the universe far
more than it owed him. To give was right; to ask
wrong. From birth he was indebted to so many, like
his father, and for so much. But you could not re-
pay the universe, or anyone, or build a career as a
Conjure Doctor on a single, brilliant spell. Talent,
Allan saw, was a curse. To have served once—was
this enough? Better perhaps never to have served
at all than to go on, foolishly, in the wreckage of
former grace, glossing over his frigidity with cheap
fireworks, window dressing, a trashy display of
pyrotechnics, gimmicks designed to distract others
from seeing that the magician onstage was dead.

Now the Sorcerer's apprentice placed his
stones and herbs into the pail, which he filled with
river water; then he built a fire behind a rock. Rags
of fog floated over the waste-clogged riverbank as
Allan drew a horseshoe in chalk. He sat cross-

legged in wet grass that smelled faintly of oil and
fish, faced east, and cursed at the top of his voice.
"I conjure and I invoke thee, O Magoa, strong
king of the East. I order thee to obey me, to send
thy servants Onoskelis and Tepheus."

Two froglike shapes stitched from the fumes
of Allan's potion began to take form above the pail.

Next he invoked the demon king of the North,
who brought Ornia, a beautiful, blue-skinned lamia
from the river bottom. Her touch, Allan knew, was
death. She wore a black gown, a necklace of dead
spiders, and entered through the opening of the
enchanted horseshoe. The South sent Rabdos, a
griffinlike hound, all teeth and hair, that hurtled
toward the apprentice from the woods; and from
the West issued Bazazath, the most terrible of all—
a collage of horns, cloven feet, and goatish eyes so
wild Allan wrenched away his head. Upriver, he
saw kerosene lamplight moving from the direction
of town. A faraway voice called, "Allan? Allan?
Allan, is that you? Allan, are you out there?" His
father. The one he had truly harmed. Allan frowned
and faced those he had summoned.

"Apprentice," rumbled Bazazath, "*student*,
you risk your life by opening hell."

"I am only that, a student," said Allan, "the
one who studies beauty, who wishes to give it back,
but who cannot serve what he loves."

"You are wretched, indeed," said Bazazath,

and he glanced back at the others. "Isn't he wretched?"

They said, as one, "Worse."

Allan did not understand. He felt Richard's presence hard by, heard him call from the mystic circle's edge, which no man or devil could break. "How am I worse?"

"Because," said the demon of the West, "to love the good, the beautiful is right, but to labor on and will the work when you are obviously *beneath* this service is to parody them, twist them beyond recognition, to lay hold of what was once beautiful and make it a monstrosity. It becomes *black* magic. Sorcery is relative, student—dialectical, if you like expensive speech. And this, exactly, is what you have done with the teachings of Rubin Bailey."

"No," blurted Allan.

The demon of the West smiled. "Yes."

"Then," Allan asked, "you must destroy me?" It was less a question than a request.

"That is why we are here." Bazazath opened his arms. "You must step closer."

He had not known before the real criminality of his deeds. How dreadful that love could disfigure the thing loved. Allan's eyes bent up toward Richard. It was too late for apologies. Too late for promises to improve. He had failed everyone, particularly his father, whose face now collapsed into tears, then hoarse weeping like some great animal with a broken spine. In a moment he would drop to both knees. Don't want me, thought Allan. Don't love me as I am. Could he do nothing right? His work caused irreparable harm—and his death, trivial as it was in his own eyes, that, too, would cause suffering. Why must his choices be so hard? If he returned home, his days would be a dreary marking time for magic, which might never come again, living to one side of what he had loved, and loved still, for fear of creating evil—this was surely the worst curse of all, waiting for grace, but in suicide he would drag his father's last treasure, dirtied as it was, into hell behind him.

"It grows late," said Bazazath. "Have you decided?"

The apprentice nodded, yes.

He scrubbed away part of the chalk circle with the ball of his foot, then stepped toward his father. The demons waited—two might still be had this night for the price of one. But Allan felt within his chest the first spring of resignation, a giving way of both the hunger to heal and the anxiety to avoid evil. Was this surrender the one thing the Sorcerer could not teach? His pupil did not know. Nor did he truly know, now that he was no longer a Sorcerer's apprentice with a bright future, how to comfort his father. Awkwardly, Allan lifted Richard's wrist with his right hand, for he was right-handed, then squeezed, tightly, the old man's thick, ruined fingers. For a second his father twitched back in an old slave reflex, the safety catch still on, then fell heavily toward his son. The demons looked on indifferently, then glanced at each other. After a moment they left, seeking better game.

FOR THE BEST IN PAPERBACKS, LOOK FOR THE

In every corner of the world, on every subject under the sun, Penguin represents quality and variety—the very best in publishing today.

For complete information about books available from Penguin—including Pelicans, Puffins, Peregrines, and Penguin Classics—and how to order them, write to us at the appropriate address below. Please note that for copyright reasons the selection of books varies from country to country.

In the United Kingdom: For a complete list of books available from Penguin in the U.K., please write to *Dept E.P., Penguin Books Ltd, Harmondsworth, Middlesex, UB7 0DA.*

In the United States: For a complete list of books available from Penguin in the U.S., please write to *Dept BA, Penguin*, Box 120, Bergenfield, New Jersey 07621-0120.

In Canada: For a complete list of books available from Penguin in Canada, please write to *Penguin Books Ltd, 2801 John Street, Markham, Ontario L3R 1B4.*

In Australia: For a complete list of books available from Penguin in Australia, please write to the *Marketing Department, Penguin Books Ltd, P.O. Box 257, Ringwood, Victoria 3134.*

In New Zealand: For a complete list of books available from Penguin in New Zealand, please write to the *Marketing Department, Penguin Books (NZ) Ltd, Private Bag, Takapuna, Auckland 9.*

In India: For a complete list of books available from Penguin, please write to *Penguin Overseas Ltd, 706 Eros Apartments, 56 Nehru Place, New Delhi, 110019.*

In Holland: For a complete list of books available from Penguin in Holland, please write to *Penguin Books Nederland B.V., Postbus 195, NL-1380AD Weesp, Netherlands.*

In Germany: For a complete list of books available from Penguin, please write to *Penguin Books Ltd, Friedrichstrasse 10-12, D-6000 Frankfurt Main I, Federal Republic of Germany.*

In Spain: For a complete list of books available from Penguin in Spain, please write to *Longman, Penguin España, Calle San Nicolas 15, E-28013 Madrid, Spain.*

In Japan: For a complete list of books available from Penguin in Japan, please write to *Longman Penguin Japan Co Ltd, Yamaguchi Building, 2-12-9 Kanda Jimbocho, Chiyoda-Ku, Tokyo 101, Japan.*

FOR THE BEST IN CONTEMPORARY AMERICAN FICTION

☐ **THE WOMEN OF BREWSTER PLACE**
A Novel in Seven Stories
Gloria Naylor

Winner of the American Book Award, this is the story of seven survivors of an urban housing project — a blind alley feeding into a dead end. From a variety of backgrounds, they experience, fight against, and sometimes transcend the fate of black women in America today.

         192 pages   *ISBN: 0-14-006690-X*   **$5.95**

☐ **STONES FOR IBARRA**
Harriet Doerr

An American couple comes to the small Mexican village of Ibarra to reopen a copper mine, learning much about life and death from the deeply faithful villagers.   *214 pages*   *ISBN: 0-14-007562-3*   **$5.95**

☐ **WORLD'S END**
T. Coraghessan Boyle

"Boyle has emerged as one of the most inventive and verbally exuberant writers of his generation," writes *The New York Times*. Here he tells the story of Walter Van Brunt, who collides with early American history while searching for his lost father.   *456 pages*   *ISBN: 0-14-009760-0*   **$8.95**

☐ **THE WHISPER OF THE RIVER**
Ferrol Sams

The story of Porter Osborn, Jr., who, in 1938, leaves his rural Georgia home to face the world at Willingham University, *The Whisper of the River* is peppered with memorable characters and resonates with the details of place and time. Ferrol Sams's writing is regional fiction at its best.

         528 pages   *ISBN: 0-14-008387-1*   **$6.95**

☐ **ENGLISH CREEK**
Ivan Doig

Drawing on the same heritage he celebrated in *This House of Sky*, Ivan Doig creates a rich and varied tapestry of northern Montana and of our country in the late 1930s.   *338 pages*   *ISBN: 0-14-008442-8*   **$6.95**

☐ **THE YEAR OF SILENCE**
Madison Smartt Bell

A penetrating look at the varied reactions to a young woman's suicide exactly one year later, *The Year of Silence* "captures vividly and poignantly the chancy dance of life." (*The New York Times Book Review*)

         208 pages   *ISBN: 0-14-011533-1*   **$6.95**

FOR THE BEST IN CONTEMPORARY AMERICAN FICTION

☐ **IN THE COUNTRY OF LAST THINGS**
Paul Auster

Death, joggers, leapers, and Object Hunters are just some of the realities of future city life in this spare, powerful, visionary novel about one woman's struggle to live and love in a frightening post-apocalyptic world.

208 pages   ISBN: 0-14-009705-8   **$5.95**

☐ **BETWEEN C&D**
New Writing from the Lower East Side Fiction Magazine
Joel Rose and Catherine Texier, Editors

A startling collection of stories by Tama Janowitz, Gary Indiana, Kathy Acker, Barry Yourgrau, and others, *Between C&D* is devoted to short fiction that ignores preconceptions — fiction not found in conventional literary magazines.

194 pages   ISBN: 0-14-010570-0   **$7.95**

☐ **LEAVING CHEYENNE**
Larry McMurtry

The story of a love triangle unlike any other, *Leaving Cheyenne* follows the three protagonists — Gideon, Johnny, and Molly — over a span of forty years, until all have finally "left Cheyenne."

254 pages   ISBN: 0-14-005221-6   **$6.95**

FOR THE BEST LITERATURE, LOOK FOR THE

☐ **A SPORT OF NATURE**
Nadine Gordimer

Hillela, Nadine Gordimer's "sport of nature," is seductive and intuitively gifted at life. Casting herself adrift from her family at seventeen, she lives among political exiles on an East African beach, marries a black revolutionary, and ultimately plays a heroic role in the overthrow of apartheid.

       354 pages ISBN: 0-14-008470-3 **$7.95**

☐ **THE COUNTERLIFE**
Philip Roth

By far Philip Roth's most radical work of fiction, *The Counterlife* is a book of conflicting perspectives and points of view about people living out dreams of renewal and escape. Illuminating these lives is the skeptical, enveloping intelligence of the novelist Nathan Zuckerman, who calculates the price and examines the results of his characters' struggles for a change of personal fortune.

       372 pages ISBN: 0-14-009769-4 **$4.95**

☐ **THE MONKEY'S WRENCH**
Primo Levi

Through the mesmerizing tales told by two characters—one, a construction worker/philosopher who has built towers and bridges in India and Alaska; the other, a writer/chemist, rigger of words and molecules—Primo Levi celebrates the joys of work and the art of storytelling.

       174 pages ISBN: 0-14-010357-0 **$6.95**

☐ **IRONWEED**
William Kennedy

"Riding up the winding road of Saint Agnes Cemetery in the back of the rattling old truck, Francis Phelan became aware that the dead, even more than the living, settled down in neighborhoods." So begins William Kennedy's Pulitzer-Prize winning novel about an ex-ballplayer, part-time gravedigger, and full-time drunk, whose return to the haunts of his youth arouses the ghosts of his past and present.   *228 pages ISBN: 0-14-007020-6* **$6.95**

☐ **THE COMEDIANS**
Graham Greene

Set in Haiti under Duvalier's dictatorship, *The Comedians* is a story about the committed and the uncommitted. Actors with no control over their destiny, they play their parts in the foreground; experience love affairs rather than love; have enthusiasms but not faith; and if they die, they die like Mr. Jones, by accident.

       288 pages ISBN: 0-14-002766-1 **$4.95**

FOR THE BEST LITERATURE, LOOK FOR THE

☐ **THE BOOK AND THE BROTHERHOOD**
Iris Murdoch

Many years ago Gerard Hernshaw and his friends banded together to finance a political and philosophical book by a monomaniacal Marxist genius. Now opinions have changed, and support for the book comes at the price of moral indignation; the resulting disagreements lead to passion, hatred, a duel, murder, and a suicide pact.   *602 pages   ISBN: 0-14-010470-4*   **$8.95**

☐ **GRAVITY'S RAINBOW**
Thomas Pynchon

Thomas Pynchon's classic antihero is Tyrone Slothrop, an American lieutenant in London whose body anticipates German rocket launchings. Surely one of the most important works of fiction produced in the twentieth century, *Gravity's Rainbow* is a complex and awesome novel in the great tradition of James Joyce's *Ulysses*.   *768 pages   ISBN: 0-14-010661-8*   **$10.95**

☐ **FIFTH BUSINESS**
Robertson Davies

The first novel in the celebrated "Deptford Trilogy," which also includes *The Manticore* and *World of Wonders*, *Fifth Business* stands alone as the story of a rational man who discovers that the marvelous is only another aspect of the real.   *266 pages   ISBN: 0-14-004387-X*   **$4.95**

☐ **WHITE NOISE**
Don DeLillo

Jack Gladney, a professor of Hitler Studies in Middle America, and his fourth wife, Babette, navigate the usual rocky passages of family life in the television age. Then, their lives are threatened by an "airborne toxic event"—a more urgent and menacing version of the "white noise" of transmissions that typically engulfs them.   *326 pages   ISBN: 0-14-007702-2*   **$7.95**

You can find all these books at your local bookstore, or use this handy coupon for ordering:

Penguin Books By Mail
Dept. BA Box 999
Bergenfield, NJ 07621-0999

Please send me the above title(s). I am enclosing _____ (please add sales tax if appropriate and $1.50 to cover postage and handling). Send check or money order—no CODs. Please allow four weeks for shipping. We cannot ship to post office boxes or addresses outside the USA. *Prices subject to change without notice.*

Ms./Mrs./Mr. _____

Address _____

City/State _____ Zip _____

Sales tax: CA: 6.5%   NY: 8.25%   NJ: 6%   PA: 6%   TN: 5.5%

FOR THE BEST LITERATURE, LOOK FOR THE

□ THE LAST SONG OF MANUEL SENDERO
Ariel Dorfman

In an unnamed country, in a time that might be now, the son of Manuel Sendero refuses to be born, beginning a revolution where generations of the future wait for a world without victims or oppressors.

464 pages   ISBN: 0-14-008896-2   **$7.95**

□ THE BOOK OF LAUGHTER AND FORGETTING
Milan Kundera

In this collection of stories and sketches, Kundera addresses themes including sex and love, poetry and music, sadness and the power of laughter. "*The Book of Laughter and Forgetting* calls itself a novel," writes John Leonard of *The New York Times*, "although it is part fairly tale, part literary criticism, part political tract, part musicology, part autobiography. It can call itself whatever it wants to, because the whole is genius."

240 pages   ISBN: 0-14-009693-0   **$6.95**

□ TIRRA LIRRA BY THE RIVER
Jessica Anderson

Winner of the Miles Franklin Award, Australia's most prestigious literary prize, *Tirra Lirra by the River* is the story of a woman's seventy-year search for the place where she truly belongs. Nora Porteous's series of escapes takes her from a small Australia town to the suburbs of Sydney to London, where she seems finally to become the woman she always wanted to be.

142 pages   ISBN: 0-14-006945-3   **$4.95**

□ LOVE UNKNOWN
A. N. Wilson

In their sweetly wild youth, Monica, Belinda, and Richeldis shared a bachelor-girl flat and became friends for life. Now, twenty years later, A. N. Wilson charts the intersecting lives of the three women through the perilous waters of love, marriage, and adultery in this wry and moving modern comedy of manners.

202 pages   ISBN: 0-14-010190-X   **$6.95**

□ THE WELL
Elizabeth Jolley

Against the stark beauty of the Australian farmlands, Elizabeth Jolley portrays an eccentric, affectionate relationship between the two women—Hester, a lonely spinster, and Katherine, a young orphan. Their pleasant, satisfyingly simple life is nearly perfect until a dark stranger invades their world in a most horrifying way.

176 pages   ISBN: 0-14-008901-2   **$6.95**

FOR THE BEST LITERATURE, LOOK FOR THE

☐ **HERZOG**
Saul Bellow

Winner of the National Book Award, *Herzog* is the imaginative and critically acclaimed story of Moses Herzog: joker, moaner, cuckhold, charmer, and truly an Everyman for our time.

342 pages   ISBN: 0-14-007270-5   **$6.95**

☐ **FOOLS OF FORTUNE**
William Trevor

The deeply affecting story of two cousins—one English, one Irish—brought together and then torn apart by the tide of Anglo-Irish hatred, *Fools of Fortune* presents a profound symbol of the tragic entanglements of England and Ireland in this century.   240 pages   ISBN: 0-14-006982-8   **$6.95**

☐ **THE SONGLINES**
Bruce Chatwin

Venturing into the desolate land of Outback Australia—along timeless paths, and among fortune hunters, redneck Australians, racist policemen, and mysterious Aboriginal holy men—Bruce Chatwin discovers a wondrous vision of man's place in the world.   296 pages   ISBN: 0-14-009429-6   **$7.95**

☐ **THE GUIDE: A NOVEL**
R. K. Narayan

Raju was once India's most corrupt tourist guide; now, after a peasant mistakes him for a holy man, he gradually begins to play the part. His succeeds so well that God himself intervenes to put Raju's new holiness to the test.

220 pages   ISBN: 0-14-009657-4   **$5.95**

You can find all these books at your local bookstore, or use this handy coupon for ordering:

Penguin Books By Mail
Dept. BA Box 999
Bergenfield, NJ 07621-0999

Please send me the above title(s). I am enclosing _____ (please add sales tax if appropriate and $1.50 to cover postage and handling). Send check or money order—no CODs. Please allow four weeks for shipping. We cannot ship to post office boxes or addresses outside the USA. *Prices subject to change without notice.*

Ms./Mrs./Mr. _____

Address _____

City/State _____ Zip _____

Sales tax: CA: 6.5%   NY: 8.25%   NJ: 6%   PA: 6%   TN: 5.5%

FOR THE BEST LITERATURE, LOOK FOR THE

☐ **VOSS**
Patrick White

Set in nineteenth-century Australia, *Voss* is the story of the secret passion between an explorer and a young orphan. From the careful delineation of Victorian society to the stark narrative of adventure in the Australian desert, Patrick White's novel is one of extraordinary power and virtuosity. White won the Nobel Prize for Literature in 1973.

448 pages   *ISBN: 0-14-001438-1*   **$7.95**

☐ **STONES FOR IBARRA**
Harriet Doerr

An American couple, the only foreigners in the Mexican village of Ibarra, have come to reopen a long-dormant copper mine. Their plan is to live out their lives here, connected to the place and to each other. Along the way, they learn much about life, death, and the tide of fate from the Mexican people around them.

214 pages   *ISBN: 0-14-007562-3*   **$6.95**